Tales of an Ashanti Father

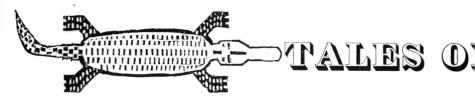

TALES O

Peggy Appiah

AN ASHANTI FATHER

Illustrated by Mora Dickson

⊕

André Deutsch

FIRST PUBLISHED 1967 BY
ANDRE DEUTSCH LIMITED
105 GREAT RUSSELL STREET
LONDON WC1
COPYRIGHT © 1967 BY PEGGY APPIAH
SECOND IMPRESSION AUGUST 1970
THIRD IMPRESSION APRIL 1974
ALL RIGHTS RESERVED
PRINTED IN GREAT BRITAIN
BY THE ANCHOR PRESS LTD
TIPTREE ESSEX

ISBN 0 233 95927 0

First published in the United States of America 1981
Library of Congress Number
80-2697

To the people of Ashanti
whose stories these are
in gratitude and affection

Contents

Introduction

KWAKU ANANSE the Spider is undoubtedly the best known rascal in West Africa. Shrewd and cunning, greedy and clever, his actions are those of a man, and he only returns to the cobwebs on the ceiling when he is in trouble and escaping punishment. His thin waist is a continual reminder of his greed and downfall but even Nyame, the Sky-God, admits that he is the cleverest of all the animals. So well-known is he that he has given his name to the whole rich tradition of tales on which so many Ghanaian children are brought up – *anansesem* – or spider tales.

The heroes of these tales are the forest animals or chiefs and people of the villages, often they are both. There is the tortoise, the magician and doctor of the forest, the reasonable man; there is the dog, stupid but loyal; the cat, mean and clever; the rat and mouse who, despite their size, reward those who help them. There is also the Lion, King of the Forest, but he is not very clever and often ends in trouble.

The stories in this book were told in Asante-Twi, the language of Ashanti, which, lying in the forest area of Ghana, is rich in tradition and culture. They have been collected with the help of both adults and children to whom they are still alive. Many were told by my husband to our own children. Such stories are not easy to translate and since there was no written Asante language, some have never been written down.

As do most story-tellers, I have undoubtedly added a bit here and there to help those outside Ghana to understand the stories. If anything has been lost or altered I ask forgiveness. I hope that they will give as much pleasure to those who read them as they have done to generations of Ashantis who have listened to them by the light of the moon or of an oil lamp, in the evenings, in the villages of Ashanti.

British nursery rhymes are shared by English-speaking peoples all over the world and are now learnt and recited in the homes of Ghana, where English has become the official language. The tales of Aesop and Grimm are told alongside those of Kwaku Ananse in schools in Ashanti, and are repeated by the children as their own. I hope that one day these Ashanti stories will also be shared by children in homes and schools of many other lands.

Let us leave the surrounding darkness and join the story-tellers in the circle beneath the trees. It is a fine night and they are waiting to begin. . . .

How Kwaku Ananse caught the Python

THERE was once a village in Ashanti that lay near the banks of a broad river. For many years the poor villagers had been troubled by an enormous python who lived in the bank of the river and preyed on man and beast. Sometimes it would be a child from the village who disappeared, sometimes a goat or sheep, and as time went on even an occasional cow would be caught as it went down to the water to drink.

The people were in despair and a big meeting was called. No one could suggest how they could get rid of the python so that, in the end, they decided to send a messenger to ask God if he would help them and save them from the monster who lived in their midst.

When God had heard the complaints of the villagers he thought a bit and then replied: 'Tell my children that the python is also a child of mine although I deplore his habits. I cannot judge between you but there is in your neighbourhood a man whom you must all know and who boasts that he is very wise. I am often tired of his boasting. Go then to Kwaku Ananse and tell him that God has asked him to help you in your troubles. Tell him as well that if he does not succeed I shall know indeed that he is not as wise as he says and that he will be punished for his boasting. If, on the other hand, he manages to rid you of the python then I shall know he is, indeed, a wise man and I will give him even more wisdom.' Thus spoke God and the messenger took back his words to the village.

Of course the villagers knew all about Kwaku Ananse who lived in a nearby village and they hastened to find him. When they came to his hut he had not yet returned from the farm but they sat down to wait for him and watched his wife Aso cooking the evening meal.

When Kwaku Ananse returned from his farm he greeted his visitors, told Aso to give them something to drink and went to take a hasty bath. Then he returned to greet them formally and to ask them the reason for their visit.

The villagers told Kwaku of their troubles and of the message from God. When they came to the part where God had said that Kwaku Ananse thought himself very wise he interrupted them: 'That is true,' said Kwaku Ananse. 'Many times has my wisdom been proved and I know I can help you easily to solve your problem.'

Then he listened to the rest of their message. When he had heard all they had to say he sat for a minute with his head in his hands, wondering how God could doubt his ability to succeed. Presently he looked up with a smile on his face. 'I think it will be easy,' he said. 'But tell me first how big is the python. Is it as long as this house?'

'Much longer,' replied the villagers.

'Is it as long as from the end of the house to the storehouse?'

'Still longer,' they said.

'Is it then as far as from this house to the Chief's palace over there?'

'That would be about the length. And you should see how fat and strong he is . . .' they added.

Kwaku Ananse smiled again and then with a more serious face spoke as follows: 'I am sure I can succeed if you do as I say. But if I fail and the python catches me then you must promise to give me a really big funeral, for I will have died in your service.'

'Of course, of course,' agreed the villagers. 'Indeed we will ask our young girls to shave their heads and we will look out a suitable kente cloth and kuduo pots and a gold ring at once.'

Kwaku Ananse was satisfied with these arrangements and asked them only to provide, early next day, plenty of mashed yam, palm oil and eggs, which they were to bring to the river bank in the morning. So the villagers returned home, and after talking a bit with his wife and children, eating the evening meal and having a calabash of palm wine, Kwaku retired peacefully for the night.

Next morning he was up very early and went into the forest with his axe to find a strong straight young tree. This he cut down, together with plenty of tough lianas (creepers) for rope, and calling his family to help him carry them he made for the village.

The villagers were waiting for him at the river bank

with dishes piled high with mashed yam, palm oil and eggs. They were so sure that the python would kill him that they had come in funeral cloths and the village drummers were practising some new song they had composed for his funeral, which went something like this: 'Kwaku Ananse came to the river, in the morning early he came to the river. He was a brave man and there was no fear in his heart, but the python is a great python . . .' and so on. He told them to go back to the village and keep quiet and that he would call them when he had succeeded. They gave one last look at him and hurried away.

Anyone who had stayed to watch Kwaku Ananse then would have wondered what he intended to do. He sat on a tree stump near the python's hole and started talking to himself; he was a good mimic and so he could easily make two voices—his own and another, deep and scornful. The python, lying in his hole, heard the following conversation:

'I'm telling you he is enormous and very beautiful. Indeed he is a fine fellow though you all seem to hate him.'

'You are lying,' said the deep voice, 'he is not big. It is just that the villagers are cowards. He could not even swallow a pig. It is the crocodile from lower down the river who comes to steal the children and the animals.'

'It is you who lie. The python is my friend. He is a fine fellow and has had many children. Is it his fault that he is hungry at times and must take a meal? The villagers do not even offer him an egg, let alone a sheep. They are a mean lot.'

'Whoever heard of a python being beautiful? He is short and ugly, you can't know him!'

Then there was the sound of blows and of running feet and the deep voice was heard no more.

The python had come to the edge of his hole to listen to this interesting discussion. Then he heard Kwaku Ananse complaining to himself: 'If the python was a gentleman he would come out and see me. Look how I have defended his honour. I would indeed like to greet him, and is it in vain that I have brought all this mashed yam, palm oil and eggs and he has not had the courtesy to come and eat them.'

Now the python was particularly fond of mashed yam, palm oil and eggs, and decided to come out and meet his defender. He slithered on to the bank, great coils of him coming up out of the water. He was so big that even Kwaku Ananse was surprised. However he greeted him calmly and with apparent joy. 'Good evening, friend python. I see that you are indeed as big and beautiful as I was saying. Did you hear me defending you to that foolish man? Indeed I have beaten him so hard that he has run away. Now do me the honour of eating the food that I have brought you and then you can tell me something of yourself.'

The python was so impatient to eat that he hardly waited for the invitation. When the dishes were empty he licked his lips and turned his head to Kwaku Ananse thanking him for his defence and for the food, and saying how surprised he was to find such a friend. Kwaku Ananse paid some more compliments and then said: 'Friend python, would you do me a favour? I have long wanted to know your exact length. Do lie yourself up against this tree I have cut to measure you, and I will show you how we measure things in our village.'

The python, well-fed and in a good temper, was anxious to do something for Kwaku so he carefully laid himself along the tree on the river bank. It was barely long enough. When he had placed himself the python asked Kwaku, 'What is the result, my friend?'

'Oh!' said Kwaku, 'I have not measured you yet. To be quite sure I have to tie you to the tree trunk with these ropes.'

Kwaku Ananse picked up the ropes he had made and talking to himself as if he was indeed counting the inches, he tied the python securely to the tree, starting at the head and finishing at the tail. Then he sat down on the tree stump and feeling behind it brought out his axe.

The python was uncomfortable and it was hot in the midday sun. 'What is my length, my friend?' he asked again. 'Hurry up and untie me as the ropes are tight and the sun hot.'

Kwaku Ananse just laughed. Then he shouted for the villagers who came running at his call. They gazed open-mouthed at the python wondering how on earth Kwaku had caught it without a battle.

Then Kwaku Ananse went up to the python, and starting at the tail he chopped it into small pieces, taking no notice of its pleadings and talk of treachery.

'There is one for the children you stole,' said Ananse.
'There is one for the sheep you have slain.'

'There is one for the goats you have swallowed.'

'There is one for the cows you have taken.'

At each cut the people cheered. Great was the rejoicing in the village and many were the gifts heaped on Kwaku Ananse.

God, watching all from above, saw how Kwaku Ananse had outwitted the python and was annoyed that this swollen-headed child of his should have earned his reward. Taking a pot of wisdom from his store he hurled it down at Kwaku Ananse. It caught him in the middle and so hard was the shot that it nearly split him in two.

And that is why, to this day, Ananse has such a narrow waist.

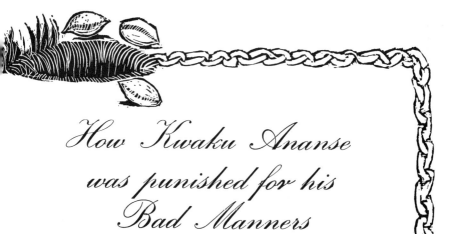

How Kwaku Ananse was punished for his Bad Manners

ONE year there had been no rain in the forest and everything was so dry that there was no food in Ananse's village. He and his family went hungry; they searched in vain for something to eat.

Now Ananse's son, Ntikuma, was growing up and was able to go and hunt for himself. One day, wandering far from the village, he came upon a big hole in the ground, and there, lying near it were three large nuts. Now Ntikuma was very hungry and realising that three nuts would not feed a family he decided to eat them himself and then go on with his search for food.

He cracked the first one carefully on a stone but it shot out of the shell and bounced into the big hole. He tried the second one, being more careful, but somehow the nut eluded him and rolled down the hole. In despair he took the third nut and swore that if he did not eat it he would go down into the hole and look for the nuts. Sure enough when the shell split the nut shot up into the air, over Ntikuma's shoulder and into the hole. He stood up and made for the hole.

Now the hole was dark and deep, but Ntikuma did not lack courage and, making himself a rope of creepers, he climbed down into the hole. To his surprise it became lighter at the bottom, and he climbed off the rope into another land.

An old woman was sitting nearby, eating nuts by the door of her hut. He greeted her politely.

'Why have you come here?' she asked.

'I was looking for food, Grandmother,' he said. 'I found three nuts but they all rolled into this hole and I came down after them.'

The old woman stared at Ntikuma, saw he was telling the truth and spoke again. 'Go behind the house. There is a big farm there and there are plenty of yams. Go and collect some, but the ones which say "Take Me" do not touch, only those which say "Do not take me". Bring me some of those and we will cook some—the others you shall take home.'

Ntikuma went into the farm and did exactly as he was told. He left the yams which asked to be taken strictly alone, and waited to find those which told him to leave them alone. At last he found these and collecting as many as he could carry he brought them back to the old lady. By now she had a fire ready and handing Ntikuma a knife she said: 'Peel off the outside carefully and put it in the pot. The inside throw away.' Ntikuma did as he was told and soon a wonderful smell came from the fire. When the meal was ready the old lady asked Ntikuma to sit down with her and gave him a bowl of food. It was delicious. Ntikuma ate quickly as he was hungry. Then he sat back to watch the old woman. He saw that she was eating through her nose. He was far too polite to remark on this and just sat and waited until she had finished. Then he said he must go home, and begged to take some yams to his mother. These the old lady willingly gave him, but first she told him to go into her room. There he would find two drums, one big and one small. He was to take the small one home with him. This he did, thanking the old woman warmly for her gifts. She told him that when he was hungry he had only to say 'cover' to the drum and food would come. So he went home to his family rejoicing.

Ntikuma told the whole story to his family after they had had the first good meal for days. His father, being jealous of his son's success, said he would go the next day and bring back something even better. He chided his son for obeying so meekly the old woman who was obviously a witch and could have given him more.

Early the next day Ananse went off to try his hand. So good were Ntikuma's directions that he easily found the spot and saw three nuts lying by the hole. 'I will follow the nuts into the hole,' he said. He cracked them right near the edge but instead of rolling in they seemed determined to stay outside. In the end he had to push the last nut in. The rope Ntikuma had made was still there and he climbed down into the hole.

Sure enough there was the old woman eating nuts. Ananse looked at her and said, 'My, what an ugly old woman you are.' But the old lady took no notice of him and went on eating nuts. Then she asked him why he had come to see her. 'Why to get food of course,' said Ananse. 'If you can give my son much, why then you must be able to give me more.'

The old lady looked at him and smiled. 'If you are so sure, then go behind the house. There is a farm there and there are plenty of yams. Do not take the ones which say "Take me" but only those which say "Do not take me".' Ananse replied, 'I am sure you are cheating me. I shall take which I please.' And he stumped off into the farm.

The first yam he saw was an enormous one. 'Take me, take me,' it cried. Ananse immediately went and cut it. But when he cut it open he found that it was full of hard nuts. Then he went further into the farm and finally found the yams which said, 'Do not take me', and collected a pile and took them back to the cottage.

The old lady had a pot boiling on the fire. She said to Ananse, 'Peel the yams carefully and throw away the inside, boiling the outside.' Ananse was angry. 'What do you take me for?' he said. 'One always cooks the inside of the yam.' And he put the inside of the yam in the pot and threw away the skin. He came back and looked in the pot and saw that it was full of stones. He had thrown the skins away, so he was forced to go to the farm and collect more yams, and to the stream and collect more water for the pot. Then he did as the old woman said.

At last they sat down to their meal. Ananse stared at the old woman, seeing she was eating through her nose. 'What a filthy habit,' he said. 'Why do you eat through your nose?' Then he laughed and laughed at the old woman. But she kept silent. Soon he pushed back his stool and said that he must go home.

The old woman watched him collect his pile of yams and then said to him, 'Before you go, go into my room. You will find two drums, one big and one small. Take the small one home with you.'

Ananse went into the old lady's room and saw a very beautiful big drum and a small plain one. 'I am not going to take the small one,' he thought. 'The big one will probably give me gold as well as food.' So he lifted the big one on his shoulder, and without giving another look at the old woman, climbed up the rope and went home.

It was with pride that Ananse put the big drum on the floor of his hut. He told the others to gather round and look at it. Then, fearing that they might take whatever treasure it produced, he asked them to go and fetch wood and water so that they could have a feast. Aso his wife and Ntikuma willingly went out to look for wood and water, wondering what wonders they would see on their return.

Kwaku Ananse sat down in front of the drum,

admiring its carvings. He went to the door to make sure no one was about. Then he sat, and said in a loud voice, 'Cover'.

Alas and alack Kwaku Ananse had taken the wrong drum. As soon as he had pronounced the magic word there was not a wonderful meal, there was not gold nor treasures, but Ananse himself saw with horror that his whole body was covered with sores and scabs. He was not fit to be seen. He cried out and ran from the house. The drum, having completed its task, disappeared. The family searched and searched for Ananse, but knowing his greed they took it for granted he had gone off to enjoy his treasure alone. It was not for many months that he returned home, bearing for always the scars of his many sores and remaining remarkably silent about his drum.

How the Rat and the Deer kept Faith with the Hunter

THERE was once a poor man, a hunter, who had had so little success in life that he was forced to go out each day to hunt in order to have enough to eat. His wife and children worked on the farms of others in exchange for fruit and vegetables, but the family never managed to save anything.

One day the hunter was out as usual and had wandered far looking for meat. At last he saw a rat sitting nibbling at a shoot in the forest. He lifted his gun, but as he did so the rat turned and called out to him: 'Please, please, don't kill me. I have a wife and children to support and I am too small to feed you or your family. Stop, I beg you.'

The hunter kept his gun in position but did not shoot. He answered the rat: 'Why should I not shoot you? I am hungry and have walked far without finding any meat.'

The rat replied: 'If you do not shoot I will work hard for you and I may be able to make you a rich man. So please save me.'

The hunter laughed at the idea of the rat being able to help him but he was kind-hearted so he called to the rat to jump into his bag and return home with him so that he could think about it. The rat climbed into his bag and away they went.

Towards evening the hunter sighted a deer in a clearing and again lifted his gun. But as he did so the deer turned and called out to him in a pitiful voice: 'Hunter, hunter, spare me, I pray, and I will help you all my life.'

'What can you do for me?' replied the hunter. 'I must eat and it is late and I have no food. I am sorry but I must shoot.'

The deer wept bitterly and begged to be spared. 'I can run swiftly, and one day you may need me to save you.'

'I have my dog who is a swift runner,' replied the hunter. But he was soft-hearted so in the end he spared the deer and asked it to return home with him whilst he thought what to do.

When they reached his home the hunter had not the heart to kill either of the animals. The rat spoke so pathetically of his family that the hunter told him to hurry home to them. But first he exacted a promise that the rat would help him to grow rich. He had almost decided to kill the deer when it looked at him with such great sorrowful eyes that he told it to go off quickly before he could change his mind.

So the hunter went supperless to bed. Since he was used to going hungry he nonetheless slept well. He awoke with the first signs of dawn and lay looking at the walls of the room as they gradually grew lighter. He wondered where he would get food that day. As he turned to get up he saw beside the pillow a large nugget of gold. He was amazed. Who could have put it there. He picked it up, turned it over and bit it. It really was gold and of the best quality. He said a heartfelt prayer to Nyame, the Sky God, thanking him for his aid, and called to his wife to hurry to the market and to buy enough food for them all to have a hearty meal.

After that, each night, a gold nugget appeared beside the hunter's pillow. He wondered who on earth could have brought it, for the doors were locked and nothing had stirred in the night.

A week later the rat came to visit the hunter in the early morning. He sat timidly on the door-step and looked all around. 'Good-morning,' he said. 'I have not been able to come before but I have come now to thank you again for saving my life. I am glad to see you looking happier. Surely you have had some good luck?'

The hunter greeted the rat and said that indeed he was feeling better but that he was a bit worried about something. It was a serious matter and one he could not expect the rat to understand.

'I am sorry you are worried, friend hunter,' said the rat. 'Let me help you to clear your worry. Maybe I could give you some advice?'

'No, little creature,' smiled the hunter. 'You would not understand these things, you have not the experience. . . .'

'Is it about the gold?' asked the rat.

'What do you know about gold?' replied the hunter, surprised and a little suspicious.

'Well, you see,' said the rat, 'I have been bringing you a gold nugget every night. I thought maybe you would want to know where it came from?'

The hunter gasped. 'How on earth do you do it?'

The rat explained that in a nearby house there lived a man who was notorious for his meanness. He pretended always to be poor and have no money but everyone knew him to be rich. He had buried his gold nuggets in the floor of his hut so that no one should find them. Thieves had indeed broken into the house at one time but nothing had been found. The rat had dug under the foundations of the house and then made a passage from the hut of the rich man to that of the hunter. Each night he carried one nugget along this passage, but it was hard work and he could not manage to carry more than that at a time.

'And,' finished the rat, 'I will go on bringing you nuggets for as long as I can. You will become a rich man as I promised. I hope that you are satisfied?'

The hunter was profuse with his thanks and happy at the thought of much more gold to come.

As time went on the villagers noticed that the hunter was looking well-fed, that his wife and children had new clothing, and that he did not seem to need to go out hunting every day any longer. He bought himself a piece of land and his family started to farm it and he was generous in entertaining his friends and helping those in need.

At the same time the rich miser was complaining
bitterly about the loss of some of his gold. At first
people did not take him seriously, for they knew he
always protested his poverty. In the end, however, they
were forced to take notice. They all went to the Chief
to discuss the matter and it was decided that all the
able-bodied men should stand guard over the house of
the miser at night to catch any thief. Night after night
they watched and night after night the miser complained of the loss of a nugget. No one was caught and
no trace of the gold was found.

The men stopped watching the hut but they talked
and wondered about the gold. The hunter kept silent

but he could not hide his added wealth. It was not in his nature to conceal his happiness. In the end the villagers began to whisper that it was he who had stolen the gold.

One morning as the hunter was preparing to leave for his farm the deer ran into his hut. It stood panting in the shadows. The hunter greeted it politely and then asked why it had not been able to help him before.

'The rat has told me what he has been able to do,' replied the deer. 'The time has now come for me to help you. As I lay resting in the forest on the edge of one of the farms I heard some of the villagers talking. They think that you have stolen the gold from the miser, and are coming to search your hut. I have run on ahead to warn you. If you bury the gold in the forest it may be found by others, if you try to hide it in your hut it may be found. Give it to me quickly and I will swallow it. Then I will come to live in your hut and you shall feed me daily with the leaves I like. If need be you can kill me and get the gold.'

The hunter hurriedly collected the gold and the deer swallowed it down. Then it asked the hunter to tie it by the leg outside the hut. No sooner had this been done than the villagers arrived and demanded to search the hunter's hut.

'But of course you may,' said the hunter and he opened up all the doors and boxes. They searched and searched and dug up the floor. But nothing did they find.

They were forced to apologise to the hunter for their mistake. He said that of course it did not matter and invited them to drink some palm wine with him so that there should be no ill-feelings.

After that no one troubled the hunter. 'Maybe,' said the Chief, 'some distant relation has left him rich. Maybe he has discovered a treasure in the forest. These are private matters and concern only him. Leave him in peace for he is harming no one.'

The rat continued to bring the gold. The deer was treated as an honoured guest and the hunter refused to kill it. 'How could I treat you in such a way,' he said, 'after what you have done for me? You have saved me from disgrace and dishonour and enabled me to continue to live happily in the village. You shall stay with me until you grow old naturally and die of old age. Then I can take your stomach and recover the gold.'

In time the deer died of old age and the hunter mourned over it and gave it a proper funeral. The people in the village wondered and gossiped. 'What a strange man,' they said, 'to fatten and feed a deer for so long and then not to eat it.'

The rat, too, was growing old. It came one day to the hunter and said; 'Friend hunter, there is very little gold left in the house of the miser. I do not like to take it all for then indeed he will be a poor man. As it is he has plenty to live on. I, too, am growing old and would like to retire. I will call on you sometimes but I think I have paid my debt in full, have I not?'

The hunter thanked the rat sincerely for all it had done. 'At any time that you require food,' he said, 'you have only to come and ask for it. You and the deer have proved faithful friends. So grateful am I to you both that I have decided that I will never again kill an animal or eat meat. You can tell your friends in the forest this, so that they will feel safe with me. Only, I beg you, ask them to keep away from my farm so that I may have good harvests.'

So the rat retired to his family and the hunter, who by now was a big land-owner, grew daily richer. His farms flourished for they were never invaded by the animals. Until he grew an old man he always spoke of the gratitude and faithfulness of the animals which far surpassed that of human beings.

The Hunter and the Tortoise

THERE was once in a village in Ashanti a very brave hunter, skilled with the gun and intrepid in the hunt. One day, as he was hunting for game in the forest, he heard afar off the sound of music. He stopped and listened and gradually crept nearer the sound until the trees thinned, and there in a clearing in the forest he saw a tortoise sitting all alone and singing gaily to the music of a small accordion.

The hunter rubbed his eyes. Never before had he seen an animal playing an instrument, let alone singing to it. He raised his gun as if to shoot and then thought better of it. With his gun raised he entered the clearing and in a loud voice addressed the tortoise.

'Tortoise,' he said, 'I could easily shoot you but I have a kind heart and instead I will take you home to my house and you shall play and sing for me there. Do you agree?' The tortoise looked him up and down and sighed. 'How can I not agree seeing that you have the gun?' he said.

The hunter went to pick him up, taking care not to damage the accordion as he did so. Just before he put the tortoise in his bag, however, it said, very seriously, 'Hunter, I warn you, I am a creature of the forest and not of the town and all my happiness is in the forest. If you take me to your home you have only yourself to blame.'

The hunter laughed and putting him in the bag set out for his village, thinking of the sensation his captive would make when he played before the Chief.

When the hunter returned to his village he went straight to see the Chief. 'Nana,' he said, 'I have found the most wonderful animal that can sing, and play the accordion. Order the gong-gong to be sounded through the village and call all your people together that they may hear this wonder.'

The Chief replied, 'If what you say is true, I will do as you ask; but make very sure before I do so for if you fool me and the people you will lose your head.' For in those days the chiefs could execute people for the slightest offence.

The hunter was so sure of himself that he asked the Chief to go ahead and call all the people. 'For,' he thought, 'the tortoise will be so grateful at having his life saved that he will play willingly for my sake.'

34

The whole village gathered together and the hunter was called and told to produce his captive. Very carefully he lifted the tortoise from his bag and put the little accordion on the ground by its side. The people stared and moved a little closer. The Hunter then asked the tortoise to play his music and to sing before the Great Chief, for it was a great honour that he should be asked to do so.

But, alas, the tortoise just blinked his beady eyes and looked stupid. He looked just a clumsy little creature from the bush with none of the magic around him necessary for him to sing. The Chief grew annoyed and the people started to mutter. The poor hunter went down on his knees and said: 'Dear tortoise, I beg you, when I saved your life in the forest when I could have killed you, I believed that you would do this little thing in return for my courtesy . . . Please, please, play your accordion and sing one of your wonderful songs.'

But the tortoise just looked stupider and turned his head away.

The people began to laugh and the Chief grew really angry. 'Oh hunter,' he said, 'I warned you I would stand no nonsense. If the tortoise does not sing at once you will have your head cut off.' And he called for the executioner.

The despairing hunter begged on in vain and presently was led away by the executioner. The crowd followed to watch, and as his head rolled on the ground they sighed and turned to look at the tortoise. The moment the hunter had been executed a change came over the little animal. He picked up the accordion and

35

in a thin piping voice he began to sing, over and over again:

'Trouble does not look for man,
It is man who looks for trouble.'

The people were amazed and the Chief even drew nearer to listen. Speaking to his Elders he said, 'The hunter was indeed to blame. He brought this creature from the bush where it was happy and thus brought about his own death.' Then, a little afraid of what the tortoise might do next he said, 'Take the tortoise back to the forest and leave him there. From now on the hunting or capturing of tortoises in the forest will be taboo to my people. Anyone who is found interfering with them will be executed.'

So the hunter was given a grand funeral—for after all he had spoken the truth—and the tortoise was returned to his clearing in the forest, where for all I know he may still be living. The villagers say that sometimes on a still night they hear the song from the forest:

'Trouble does not look for man,
It is man who looks for trouble.'
'*Asem mpe nnipa,*
Nnipa na pe asem.'

The Left-handed King

THERE was once a country which had many small kingdoms and whose kings lived in peace and friendship with each other. There were the kingdoms of Yaw, of Kwasi and of Kwaku, and the kingdoms of Kwadwo and Kwabena.

Since the country was at peace many travellers visited the kingdoms and as they travelled from one to the other they would bear with them tales and reports of their journeyings. King Kwadwo was wont to listen to these travellers for he liked to hear all about his neighbours. Whenever he heard the tales they seemed to be mostly about King Kwabena and his kingdom, how wonderful everything was there and how prosperous and happy the people were.

After a time King Kwadwo called his councillors together. When they were assembled he asked them if they knew why it was that everyone brought tales of King Kwabena's kingdom and what it was that made it better than all the others. The councillors shook their heads and one after the other they pleaded ignorance.

'Very well, then,' said King Kwadwo, 'I will go and visit the kingdom myself and see what it is that makes it better than all others.' So he sent forth ambassadors to King Kwabena and asked if he might pay him a visit. King Kwabena was delighted and very soon King Kwadwo was on his way, accompanied by courtiers and gifts. The councillors were left behind to rule the kingdom.

When King Kwadwo reached the Kingdom of Kwabena he was greeted with great pomp and ceremony. The people all came out to cheer him and there was

much drumming and dancing. He saw how happy and prosperous the kingdom looked.

For many days King Kwadwo stayed with King Kwabena. There was feasting and music, sports and hunting in the forest, and all the time King Kwadwo asked questions about how the kingdom was ruled. But try as he would in no way could King Kwadwo see that the laws of the country differed from his own. The more he looked about him the more puzzled he grew.

At last, when King Kwadwo was having a banquet with King Kwabena, he noticed that the King ate with his left hand—his right arm being covered with his cloth. As time went on he came to the conclusion that it must be this eating with the left hand which had been responsible for the good rule and happiness in the kingdom. He returned home determined to imitate this habit so that he too might be famous.

When King Kwadwo returned home he was welcomed by his councillors and people. At once he beat the gong-gong and called all the people together. He told them of his successful visit, of the happiness and prosperity of King Kwabena's kingdom. At last he said, 'I have decided that all this success comes from one thing—King Kwabena eats with his left hand. From now on I order all the people of my realm to eat with their left hands. Then we, too, will be famous. Do you all agree?'

Now, in many places, as today, it was considered rude to eat with your left hand, to point the way with it or to accept or give gifts with it, so the change would be a very serious one. However, the people of King Kwadwo's kingdom were not used to thinking for themselves. They did what they were told and had given up thinking about it. King Kwadwo himself was a dictator and though he always pretended to consult his people he ended up by doing exactly what he wanted.

So when again he asked his advisers if they would agree to use their left hands they shouted, 'Yes, yes, that is a good idea.'

There was, however, one old, old man who stood by shaking his head. When all the others cheered and shouted, 'Yes, yes,' he alone stood silent. The King, seeing him standing there sent someone to ask him why he did not rejoice with the others.

Slowly the old man hobbled up to the King. 'I cannot agree, O King!' he said—and the people gasped at his audacity.

The King was angry but considering the old man's age only demanded an explanation. The old man replied: 'When you visited the Kingdom of Kwabena, Your Majesty, did you not enquire why he used his left hand? Did you not ask him for the reason? Surely you did not come to this serious decision without asking this question?' The old man was silent.

The King was now very angry, but sensing that it would be unwise to silence the old man, he replied roughly: 'Why do I need to ask? Is not the prosperity of his kingdom proof enough? Since this was the only difference I could see between our kingdoms I knew that it must be the reason.'

'Alas,' said the old man, 'that you should copy things without asking for the reason and knowing the circumstances. Let me tell you a tale. Many years ago when I was a young man I travelled through the Kingdom of Kwabena. It was in the time of his uncle. When I came to the capital of the Kingdom I found it in turmoil. Young Kwabena, scarcely out of his childhood, had persuaded the hunters to take him out after lion. A lion had been wounded and turned on the hunters, who were not in time to save Kwabena from being bitten in the arm. In time his arm withered and he lost his hand. That is why King Kwabena eats with his left hand. He has no right hand!'

The old man was silent.

The councillors who had heard the tale turned to the King. 'King Kwadwo,' they said, 'you have wronged us. You have ordered your people to do a difficult thing without knowing the reason why. You have copied blindly the acts of another man. You are not fit to be King.'

King Kwadwo knew not what to say. With the people behind them his councillors were able to remove him from the throne and asked the old man to act as regent until they could find a wiser and more suitable ruler.

Why the Leopard has Spots

ONE day the ant's mother died and all the animals decided to accompany him to the funeral which was at some distance from their village.

As they went along the road from the village they passed a garden-egg farm, a farm full of wonderful, ripe garden-eggs. Now the leopard was particularly fond of garden-eggs, indeed he doted on them. His mouth watered when he saw them and as he passed the farm he went slower and slower until he was the last animal in the procession. Then he sat down in the path and thought. Soon he was alone. He looked carefully round and seeing no one he whipped round and rushed into the farm.

He ate and he ate and he ate, until nearly half of the farm had been consumed. Then he could eat no more and went slowly off along the path to join the other animals.

As luck would have it the farmer arrived just after

he left and seeing all the animals passing along the road ran after them and began to curse and swear at them for having stolen his food. Of course the animals denied having stolen the garden-eggs and many were indignant at the accusation. They stopped to argue and the farmer demanded that they should stand trial. This they willingly agreed to do—provided it did not take too long or they would be late at the funeral.

The farmer quickly made a great fire in a hollow in the ground and told the animals to jump over it. 'If you are innocent,' he said, 'you will not be harmed, but the guilty one will fall into the fire.'

One after another the animals leapt over the flames, some of them singing a song to get up their courage before they jumped. At last only the leopard was left. Everyone expected him to cross the now smouldering embers easily. He sang one song. He started another; the animals were impatient to go on to the funeral and shouted at him to hurry. He got ready to spring but— maybe it was the garden-eggs in his stomach, maybe it was his nerves. The animals saw him leap into the air, but instead of coming down on the other side he fell right into the middle of the smouldering embers. He howled and rushed from the fire, rolling on the ground, but the fire had burnt patches in his fur, some black, some brown. The animals stared in amazement and then scolded the leopard as a thief. The farmer felt he had had enough punishment and left him alone to crawl back home, shamed before all the others.

And so to this day the leopard carries a spotted coat, a perpetual reminder of his greed.

How Kwaku Ananse became Bald

THERE was once a kingdom, ruled over by the leopard, whose citizens were almost all farmers. It was a small but happy kingdom, for the leopard was a wise ruler and the people were content to do as he ordered.

For many years the farmers prospered and lived in honesty and friendship with each other. Then, suddenly, a sad thing happened. One after another the farmers complained that someone was coming in the night and stealing food from their farms. They wondered who on earth it could be, for were they not all farmers, and farmer does not steal from farmer. In the end they sent a delegation to see the King.

The King listened seriously to their complaints, watching their faces as he did so. Then he asked them to make suggestions as to how they should catch the thief, and what they should do to him.

The donkey suggested that he be made to work all his life for the farmers from whom he had stolen; some others suggested a whipping round the town; and Kwaku Ananse said he would recommend that the thief be made bald, so that all men would recognise him. He said he knew how this could be done. The King did not listen very hard to the suggestions, for he was wondering what course he should take. The little tortoise, however, sitting quietly in a corner, heard and remembered all.

In the end it was decided that the farmers would wait to see if the meeting had acted as a warning to the thief, or if further thefts would occur.

A few days later Kwaku Ananse came running to the King. 'O King,' he cried. 'Someone has stolen half the produce of my farm. What am I to do?'

'What do you advise, Ananse?' asked the King.

'I would beat the gong-gong and announce that if ever this happens again the thief will meet with the most severe punishment. If we do that,' said Ananse, 'I am sure there will be no more thefts for a week or so, as the thief will be too frightened. After three weeks let us start to watch out again.'

'I agree,' said the King. 'We will again wait and see.'

Now the King was a very intelligent animal. For long he had been the best hunter in the forest—for who could hunt better than the leopard? He thought it odd that when Kwaku Ananse's farm had been robbed no one else suffered, whereas before that it was the other farmers, and not Ananse, who had lost things. He thought it strange, too, that Ananse should suggest that nothing be done for three weeks. So when he was sure that Kwaku Ananse had returned to his farm, he called his most trusted soldiers. To them he said: 'Soldiers, I think that this night the thief will strike

45

again. Pretend to be going early to bed and then come to me here and I will tell you what to do.'

That night the soldiers came quietly to the palace of the King, and he told them to go round all the farms as silently as possible and see if they could catch anyone.

The soldiers went into the forest. It was dark as the clouds scudded across the moon, doubly dark in the forest. But the soldiers were used to finding their way about, and they listened all the more carefully.

In the middle of the night they paused for a moment in a forest clearing. Then from afar off they heard the sound of heavy footsteps. They hid behind the trees, and into the clearing came a heavily-laden creature. A huge pile of cassava roots almost hid the bearer.

The soldiers jumped out and caught the thief by the arms. The load toppled off his head and there stood Kwaku Ananse, trembling with fright.

'Heh! Kwaku Ananse,' said the soldiers. 'So you are the thief. You are in trouble. Just you wait till we take you to the King and then see what will become of you.' And they dragged him away with them.

Ananse begged and beseeched them to let him go, to save him and his family from disgrace. He swore it was his first offence, and he offered them all his farm and his money—everything he could think of—for his freedom.

The soldiers only dragged him all the faster. 'We are loyal to the King,' they said. 'How dare you try and corrupt us.'

When they reached the palace the soldiers woke up the King, and he ordered the gong-gong to be beaten immediately and the people to be called to the palace. So, in the light of early morning, all the people came trooping to the palace where Kwaku Ananse stood in chains in the courtyard.

When the people had collected, the King addressed them: 'Here is your thief, O people. What do you wish me to do to him?'

'Kill him!' shouted some.

'No,' said the King. 'We have no capital punishment here, and I do not wish to shed blood.'

Then everyone started shouting different suggestions till the King called for order. 'One at a time,' he said.

The little tortoise had made his way to the front of the crowd, and managed to catch the King's eye.

'Friend tortoise,' he said, 'have you a suggestion to make?'

'Yes, Your Majesty,' said the tortoise. 'Do you remember that at our first meeting Kwaku Ananse himself made a suggestion as to how we should punish the culprit?'

'I have forgotten,' said the King. 'Tell me.'

'He said that we should make the thief bald for life, so that all men could recognise him?'

Kwaku Ananse, who had perhaps feared an even worse punishment, felt a little happier.

'That is a good idea, friend tortoise,' said the King. 'Do you not think so, Kwaku Ananse?'

Ananse could hardly refuse to accept a punishment he himself had suggested. 'I agree,' he whispered.

'Tell us how it is done, Kwaku Ananse, and we will proceed with the punishment,' said the King.

So Kwaku Ananse was forced to reveal his secret. He told them to boil some palm oil and brush it all over the head. 'Then,' he said, 'all the hair will fall out and never grow again.'

So the King ordered that palm oil be boiled, and his soldiers brushed it into Kwaku Ananse's hair. His screams reached the furthest ends of the village.

It was as he said—all his hair fell out. From that day to this all spiders have been bald.

Kwaku Ananse sorrowfully taught his children that: 'A doctor should always be prepared to take his own medicine.'

The Tortoise and the Hare

THE Lion, King of Beasts, once called all the creatures of his kingdom together and when even the smallest and the slowest had arrived he addressed them thus:

'My people, I have long been concerned by the lack of unity and co-operation amongst the animals. Not only do we suffer the depradations of hunters and trappers but animal attacks animal in the forest and you, my people, have ceased to help each other. Were we all to work together no hunter would be able to attack us, and when groups of men tried to come into the forest we would have adequate warning and would be able to keep out of their way, and even to destroy

them. What suggestions have you so that we should work better together?'

One animal after another stood up and talked, some making suggestions and some complaining that it was not their fault. The little tortoise sat at the feet of the King and watched and listened. After a bit the hare jumped up and when the King had nodded that he could speak he said. 'I, O King, do not need help. I can run and jump and am quite capable of looking after myself. As you know I am the swiftest animal in the forest. If anyone starts to chase me I can tire him out. When any of us are caught it is just by accident. I am quite happy with things as they are.'

Then all the animals started to talk at once and the King was obliged to silence them. He caught the eye of the little tortoise and seeing he wanted to speak, he lifted him up on a stool so that the other animals could see him.

The tortoise looked round the crowd and turned to the hare. Then he began to speak: 'You hare, you are a foolish animal. Have you not heard that the King advises that we work more together. You think you are safe but even I, the little tortoise, could beat you in a race and therefore teach you the importance of unity and co-operation.'

The hare was furious and shouted back, 'You silly little creature. You know quite well that you could not even begin to race with me. I am the swiftest animal of the forest and you are known for your slowness. You insult me by your talk. You had better take back what you said.'

The tortoise smiled. 'If you are so sure of yourself then I will race you and show you that I can win,' he said.

The hare, angrier than ever, addressed the King who was smiling broadly at the idea of the tortoise racing.

'O King,' said the hare. 'I challenge the tortoise to prove what he says or else he should be punished. I ask you to arrange for a race tomorrow.'

The King agreed and soon the animals were marking out the course of the race and talking and laughing about the tortoise's challenge. Indeed, they laughed so much that the sound could be heard in the next village.

The time was fixed for the race and the animals went home. The tortoise hurried to his house and sent out messengers to fetch all the members of his family, young and old. When they had arrived and the doors of the yard were closed against strangers, the tortoise addressed them thus.

'Members of my family, elders and friends, you will have heard of the rudeness of the hare and of my challenge to him. I have called you together because this is a matter that affects not only myself but the honour of every tortoise. If I win then glory will go to our family as a whole; if I lose, as I do not intend to do, then we are all disgraced. Will you all help me so that I can win?'

The largest and oldest of the tortoises replied, 'What you say is true and we will all help. Nonetheless we think you very unwise to challenge the hare in this matter for you cannot possibly beat him.'

'There, Grandfather, you are wrong,' replied the tortoise. 'With your help I shall win. Listen now to what I have to tell you, and do as I say. Will all the tortoises of my size and colour please come to this side.'

There was a scuffling and a large body of the tortoises moved across the yard. 'Each one of you has a part to play. I will give you all numbers and you will know your order,' said the tortoise, and he numbered them all.

'Now number one,' he said, 'you go and hide in the bush some fifty feet from the beginning of the course. When the race has started and you see the hare approaching, step out into the path and start going along the path. At the same time I will disappear into the bush, so that when the hare turns round he will see no one on the path. Number two, you go some forty feet further on . . .' And the tortoise gave them all their places along the route. The last one he gave special instructions to make sure he crossed the line ahead of the hare. Then he told them to go and take up their positions under cover of dark. He also told them that they should sing the following song when they saw the hare coming so that the next one of them would be ready to come out of the bush:

'*Me de boko-boko be duru abrokyire.*'
'With patience and diligence, I shall reach far off places.'

The following day all the animals were out early to watch the race and there was an air of festivity about.

53

When they saw the tortoise they laughed: 'He, ho, ho, hee, hee, hee, ha, ha, ha.' But the tortoise only smiled back at them.

The hare had been so angry at the insult that he had not slept all night. He had lain fuming on his bed, unable to eat or sleep. Now he was longing to be off and to prove once and for all what a fool the tortoise was.

The King had appointed judges and some stood at the beginning, some at the end of the course. At last, they were ready to start. The hare shot ahead without looking back, then, thinking it was stupid to get hot when the tortoise could not even do more than amble along, he slowed down.

About forty feet from the start the hare turned round but was surprised to see no sign of the tortoise. Then he looked ahead again and there in the middle of the path was the tortoise going along for all it was worth.

'So, you have magic,' thought the hare and he started to run more swiftly. When he turned to look again there was no tortoise behind him. He looked ahead and there in the path was the tortoise, singing a song and so bespattered with dew that it looked as if it was sweating profusely. The hare began to get angry and hurled insults at the tortoise as he passed.

Then he really began to get worried. He ran as swiftly as he could but always ahead of him in the path was the little tortoise, singing as he went:

'With patience and diligence, I shall reach far off places.'

Making a final effort the hare threw himself across the winning line, but just before he did so he heard a great cheer and people began to shout, 'The tortoise has won, the tortoise has won.' The hare collapsed groaning on the ground whilst the Judges clustered round the tortoise congratulating him.

'That was nothing,' said the tortoise, 'I am not even hot.'

The judges went at once to tell the King the result of the race. At first he would not believe them but with so many witnesses he could not fail to be convinced. He laughed heartily and again called together all the animals so that he could honour the tortoise.

When the animals had come together they called for the tortoise. In he came at the head of all his family and relations. They waddled proudly in, each one feeling and looking like a small chief. The tortoise's victory had made them proud and confident.

The King called the tortoise to come up beside him and then called on the people to cheer the victor. When the crowd was again silent the King asked the tortoise how it was that he had managed to beat the hare who was the swiftest animal in the forest.

'It was the triumph of unity and co-operation,' said the tortoise. 'We won because we all stuck together.'

'*We* won?—You mean you won,' said the King.

'Well, yes, Your Majesty, I won. You see every member of my family gave me their support so we were able to win.'

'Why do you keep saying we?' asked the King. 'It was surely you alone that won the race? Now we will call on hare to congratulate you,' and he turned to look for the hare.

The hare had been so ashamed of himself that he had slunk home and had not come to the meeting. When the King found that he was absent he sent for him and for all the members of the hare family to come quickly.

Very soon, with his head bowed, hare came into the courtyard. The other animals tittered and smiled behind their paws. Behind hare came all his people looking angry and ashamed.

One by one they were made to come up and congratulate tortoise and his family on the victory. Then the King asked the tortoise again to say how he had won the race. 'All my friends helped me,' said the tortoise.

The King being wise did not ask any more questions in public, but you may be sure that by evening he had heard the whole story. In the meantime he again addressed his people: 'The tortoise,' he said, 'has showed us the value of unity and co-operation. Let us learn from him. If you cannot all work together at least let those of the same family help each other.'

From that day many of the animals started to move together in herds for their mutual protection, the birds flew in flocks and the ants, who already knew what could be done by mutual help, moved into even greater colonies. Only the hare, embittered by his experience, continued to live alone and to rely on his speed to save him from his enemies.

Why Nephews inherit Property in Ashanti

LONG, long ago—so long that customs were not as
they are today—there lived in Ashanti a man called
Kwaku Amponsa. He and his sister, Amma Foriwaa,
had grown up together in the village and loved each
other dearly. However, as Kwaku Amponsa grew to
manhood he married and had a family and as often
happens he saw less of his sister. Nevertheless, they
remained devoted to each other.

One year Kwaku Amponsa had a run of bad luck.

His crops failed, a tornado destroyed his house, his children were sick and could not work, so at last he had to borrow money to support the family.

It was the custom in those days for those who could not pay their debts to be dragged into slavery. They were forced to work for the creditor for as long as he considered suitable to pay off the debt. Sometimes, too, they were sold abroad for their debts and never returned.

Kwaku Amponsa had been lucky to borrow money from a friend and the man was very patient. Again and again Kwaku Amponsa promised to pay him but when the day came there was no money available. At last the man said to him: 'Kwaku, I have been very patient, no friend could do more. If by next week you cannot pay me, you must come and work for me instead.' To this Kwaku was forced to agree.

The next week Kwaku still had no money so the man came and told him to pack up his things and go with him to work. Kwaku's wife cried and wailed in vain, calling upon his friend to have mercy: 'Fancy taking off an old man like that, shame on you! Have you no mercy? Have you no pity on his grey hairs? Cannot you take a younger man?'

The man turned to the wife and said, 'Very well, if you insist I will take your son to work for me instead. He is young and strong and will do the work quicker.'

The mother was horrified. 'No, no,' she cried, 'you cannot take my son. I will not have my son working as a slave. Rather take the old man, for after all the debt is his.' And she went back into the house.

The old man sighed and picking up his bundle followed his friend along the path. As luck would have it they had to pass the sister's house and Kwaku Amponsa asked permission to say farewell to her.

When Amma Foriwaa heard what had happened she cried out in consternation. 'Wait, wait, my brother. I cannot let you go like this. I too have a son. Wait only a few minutes and I will fetch him and send him in your place.' She was as good as her word. She ran off and called her son who quickly collected his things and, waving goodbye, went off with the creditor. Amma Foriwaa accompanied her brother home and gave his wife a good scolding for refusing to let their son help her husband.

Freed from his debt and cheered by the help of his sister and nephew, Kwaku Amponsa worked very hard that year. His farm prospered and soon he had enough money to send and redeem his nephew.

When the boy returned home there was great rejoicing and Kwaku Amponsa boasted to all about the behaviour of his sister and nephew. In front of all the villagers he announced that when he died his property should go to his nephew who had helped him in his extremity rather than to his ungrateful wife and children.

The villagers, too, were full of admiration for the behaviour of the sister and gave a feast in her honour. They thought of the way their own families had behaved, and after long discussion decided that in future, in all their families, the nephew should succeed to the property.

Since that day in Ashanti, and indeed in all Akan lands, it is the nephews who have inherited from their uncles—in perpetual memory of the generosity of Amma Foriwaa and her son.

Kwaku Ananse and the Unknown Assignment

THERE was once a King who ruled his people with wisdom but he loved beautiful possessions. Travellers had often told him how Death had in his Kingdom a wonderful pair of gold sandals and a golden broom. These the King coveted, though he seldom told his desires for he knew that no one could visit Death and return from his country.

In the same kingdom in a small village lived Kwaku Ananse, together with his wife Aso and his son Ntikuma. He was very clever and many people came to him for advice. The King was even a little jealous of him for the junior chiefs often went to consult Ananse instead of going to the palace. Ananse's advice was often good so many great men looked upon him as the wisest man in the land. But Kwaku Ananse wanted more than wisdom. He wanted power. One day he thought of a plan to obtain it.

In the evening Ananse sat under a tree and when he saw some of the servants of the King's palace sitting around he started to boast to them. 'I am the wisest man in the land. Why I could get the King anything he wanted, even without knowing first what it was!' After he had talked a bit in this way he saw that one of the servants had slipped away and he knew his work was done.

The next day the King sent for Ananse. When he reached the King's presence and had done obeisance he waited for the King to speak. 'Kwaku Ananse,' he said, 'I have heard of your boasts and how you set yourself up to be wiser than I. Very well then, I will make a bargain with you. I will tell a few of my advisers what I want you to do but I will not tell you yourself. Then I will give you one month to do it. If you succeed I will give you part of my kingdom to rule. If you fail you will die.' Ananse, to the King's surprise, agreed at once to this plan and bowing his way out, departed. The King then called three of his most trusted Elders and told them that he wanted Ananse to fetch him the golden sandals of Death and the golden broom with which Death swept his rooms. He smiled to himself, 'for,' he thought, 'if Ananse fails he will die; if he finds out what I want he is sure to die too, for no one ever returned from the house of Death.'

Kwaku Ananse had already laid his plans. He went back to the village and called together all the birds. He told them he had just come from the Royal Palace and had been asked to do something very beneficial to them all, but so secret that he must not tell what it was. Since he had helped many of them in the past with advice he was sure they would help him now. From each he asked one of their most beautiful feathers.

They willingly agreed. When they had departed Kwaku asked Aso, his wife, to glue the feathers to him and together with Ntikuma she soon so covered him with feathers that he could not be recognised. They did their work well and he looked so handsome that Aso thought with a sigh it was a pity he was not always like that.

So well had they done their work, too, that with a little practice he found he could fly well. He said good-bye to his family and told them that he was going somewhere for a time. Then he went to find out what the Chief wanted.

He flew straight to the royal palace. The Chief was sitting under the great shade tree in his yard and holding a meeting of all his Elders. Ananse flew onto the shade tree and flapped his wings so that the people looked up. He perched there listening whilst the people admired his beauty and asked what manner of bird it could be. One after another they shook their heads and said that never had they seen such a bird. The Chief then spoke. 'It is a pity I have sent Kwaku Ananse to Mr Death's to bring me his golden broom and sandals. Otherwise I am sure he would have told us the name of this bird. Let us catch it and keep it.' But as soon as Ananse had heard what the Chief wanted he flew off, and finding a quiet corner removed all the feathers. He went home again and told Aso to prepare things for a journey as he had to travel at once.

Aso was a wonderful cook and when Ananse asked her to prepare mashed plantain mixed with palm oil to last him some days, she made the most appetising packet and wrapped it in cocoa-yam leaves and tied it in a strong piece of cloth. Then Ananse set off for the town of Mr Death, from which no one had ever returned. But he went with a light heart, relying on his own wisdom to see him through.

He came to a small stream running through a marshy clearing. He stopped by its side and sat on a stone and opened his packet of plantain. The stream, smelling the good food, begged to be given some. At first Ananse was unwilling then he thought that if he returned that way the stream might be able to help him. So he gave it a generous portion and crossing over went on his way.

A little further on he met some driver ants. Smelling the food in his packet they begged for some. Ananse had asked Aso for some sugar to take with him and this he sprinkled liberally around. Then he promised that if they would wait there the next day he would bring them more, and he went on his way.

At last he reached the city and house of Death. Only the family of Death lived there. Mr Death was very pleased to have a visitor for, since it was well-known that visitors were always eaten, those who came, came only through ignorance or when forced to, and they were always a welcome meal. He prepared a fine meal for Kwaku Ananse and showed him to his room. Then he went back to his own and waited for Ananse to sleep so that he could kill him. But Ananse did not sleep. He lay on his mat wide awake and listened to the night sounds. Somewhere far away a tree-bear was crying and all around insects were humming and screeching. There were rats in the thatch of the roof. Presently he heard the footsteps of Mr Death. He saw the door open and Mr Death came in. 'Why are you not asleep?' he asked.

'Alas, I cannot sleep without gold sandals, and I have left mine behind,' replied Ananse. Death thought that it was odd of Ananse to want gold sandals, still, since he would get them back when Ananse was dead, there was no harm in lending his. So he went and fetched his own gold sandals and Ananse put them on. All that night Ananse lay awake and from time to time Death came to the door and called to see if he was asleep. When the morning came Death went sadly off to have his bath, thinking that Ananse could not possibly stay awake another night.

After breakfast Death sat lazing in his armchair on the stoop. He was chewing a chewing stick and still thinking of how good Ananse would taste when Ananse himself strolled up. He too had bathed and eaten and carried under his arm the golden slippers. Ananse noticed a tsetse fly on Mr Death's chair and said to him quickly, 'Mr Death, quickly, bring your golden broom. There is a tsetse fly on your chair trying to bite you. We must kill it, for if it bites so early in the day it will bring you bad luck.'

So Death went and fetched his broom and handed it to Ananse and they both kept still, watching for the fly. Presently it came back and settled on Death's knee. Ananse made as if to hit it with the broom, but missed deliberately and the fly flew off across the yard.

With the golden slippers under his arm and the

broom in his hand he chased the fly. Death sat watching in the chair. Soon Ananse turned the corner of the house and seeing that Death did not follow he made off for all he was worth. He had gone some way when unfortunately Death's son saw him running and went to tell his father.

Then the chase started. Death was very swift and would ordinarily have caught Ananse. However, soon they came to the place where the ants were waiting for Ananse. Now everyone knows that ants are the favourite food of Death and when he saw them he could not resist stopping. So sure was he he could catch Ananse that he even sent his son for a pan and they cooked the ants and ate them on the spot. In the meantime Ananse was running as fast as he could. Soon, out of breath, he came to the stream and as he jumped across he begged it to help him as it had promised. The stream started to overflow its banks and the whole clearing was filled with a wide river. Death and his son, having eaten the ants came rushing after Ananse, but they were too late. When they came to the banks of the stream and looked across they realised they had no hope of following Ananse without a boat. Much time was lost while Death's son ran back for a canoe. Despite the efforts and haste of his entire household much more time had passed when the canoe arrived. They landed on the other bank but the forest was silent and they could find no trace of Ananse. The grass had straightened up again where he had passed, and birds and animals kept well away from the family of Death. So Death and his family returned home, angry at losing their treasures, and Death never made the mistake of trusting his visitors again.

As for Ananse, he reached his village and changed his cloth. He shaved and rested and hearing no more of Death he sent a message to the Chief saying that he had arrived with what he had sent him for and that he would bring the treasures next day.

Early next morning he set out for the palace. Wrapped in a clean cloth he carried the golden sandals and the broom. He was met by messengers of the Chief and his people. The Chief himself was sitting in state in his Palace.

Ananse went before the Chief and laying the cloth on the ground he undid the knots and drew back the covering. There lay the golden sandals and the broom of Death.

The Chief was indeed surprised. He called to his Elders to come and look at the treasure. He put on the sandals and handed the broom to the Keeper of the Chief's Treasure. Then he turned to Ananse.

'Your boasts were true,' he said. 'You are indeed a wise man and you deserve your reward. You shall be put in charge of half the Kingdom'. Then he told Ananse about the beautiful bird that had visited the palace and asked if he knew its name. Ananse thought for a moment and said, 'They call it *Sewante a sankotie* —meaning, "If at first you do not hear go back and listen again".' This is one of the wise proverbs of the Akan people and it is used by the old and wise to this day.

Abena and the Python

THERE was once, in a village in Ashanti, a very beautiful girl called Abena. So beautiful was she that all the young men for miles around used to come and court her. But, alas, she had a bitter tongue and the more they told her that she was beautiful the ruder she was to them.

To the one she would say, 'What, marry you, you are much too fat, you could not possibly work,' to another, 'You, you are far too thin, people will not treat you with respect.'

She scoffed at the hunters as mere bushmen; the farmers she teased for always having their faces to the ground; the poor men she ignored for their poverty and the rich men she found ugly, or ill-mannered.

Abena's mother was a good and humble woman and her daughter's behaviour put her to shame. In vain she pleaded with Abena to choose one of the worthy suitors who sought her hand. 'Who are you,' she asked, 'to be so high and mighty? Do not your ancestors come from this village, and though we are a good old family we are not even royals? Why should you behave in such a way and put disgrace on us?'

Abena only laughed and when the nephew of a big chief from a neighbouring town next sought her hand she ridiculed him to such an extent that he went away furious.

Some way away on the banks of a river lived a very large python who was possessed of much magic. He heard of the beauty of the girl and of the way she treated her suitors and he decided that he would go and win her hand. He went towards the village and when he was nearly there he performed some magic signs and turned himself into a handsome prince, dressed in cloth of gold. The golden prince made his way to the village and the people stared at his beauty and bowed before him.

When the prince reached Abena's house he asked her parents if he might see her. They asked the handsome stranger to sit down and called to Abena who was admiring herself in a mirror in her room. She came out reluctantly, but when she saw the Prince her face changed. She came towards him looking radiant and without even waiting to be asked she told her parents that this was the man she wished to marry.

The prince was charming; he paid Abena many compliments and asked if he could marry her at once. The parents were delighted for they had feared that she would never make up her mind to marry. The prince gave them much gold and very soon the wedding festivities were under way.

When the wedding was over the prince asked

Abena's parents to collect together much food as the journey to his palace was a long one and they would need it on the way. So the parents called some thirty young girls to help carry the loads and the party was soon on its way, with many sheep and goats, much plantain and yam—in fact enough food for a month at least.

When they had left the village, but had not yet left the farms that Abena knew so well, the prince asked them to stop as he was hungry and needed a meal. Then he swallowed some four sheep, a goat, some yam and plantain, and ended up with a pineapple. Then they went on their way.

Two hours later the prince again called on them to halt as he was hungry. He ate three goats, a small pig, cassava, pawpaw and corn. Then they went on their way.

Two hours later the prince again called a halt as he was hungry. He ate three pigs, a sheep, a goat and all the bananas. Then they went on their way.

And so it went on. Abena, who had been chatting gaily when they left, watched her husband eat with amazement and gradually grew silent. At last she said, 'Husband, dear husband, if you go on eating at this rate we shall have nothing left to finish the journey.'

'I can't help it, I am hungry,' said the prince, and he took another meal.

Soon there was nothing left and when they stopped again and the prince asked for food Abena told him there was none left. 'Then I shall have to eat the maids,' he said.

By the end of the second day the prince had eaten all the maids and only Abena remained. Luckily they had come to the river near his home. When they reached its banks the prince showed Abena a large hole under the roots of a tree in the river. 'There is the entrance to my palace,' he said. 'Go in there, for it is here that we shall live.'

Abena was terrified. 'Dear husband,' she said, 'surely you are joking. Who could possibly live in such a place? I am tired with the journey, please do not tease me.'

The prince laughed. 'You can wash yourself and your garments before you go in, if you like,' he said.

Abena, to gain time, removed her cloth and started to wash it in the river. The prince turning into the python again quickly climbed the tree above her. When Abena looked round there was no one to be seen. She bent over again and as she did so the python spat at her from the branch above. The spit landed in the middle of her back and again she turned. This time she looked above and saw the prince sitting on the branch above. She was angry. 'Did you dare to spit on me?' she said, and shook her fist. The prince laughed. 'Of course,' he said. Then he climbed down the tree.

'Go into the hole,' he ordered.

'I won't,' said Abena.

'Very well, we shall see what we shall see.'

Almost immediately Abena felt strange things in her body and as she looked at her hands they grew bent and wrinkled. She leant over the water and saw

the face of an old hag. She stumbled and fell and felt that she was dying: 'Please, please my husband, don't do this to me. I will do all you say, I will obey your every word, only let me be young again.'

The prince spat again and Abena grew youthful, but she no longer dared to disobey him, and she crept weeping into the hole in the river.

Each day the python, who no longer bothered to turn himself into a prince, would come out of his hole and turning to Abena would say: 'Abena, I am going hunting to get you some meat. So don't you dare stir from the hole until I come back, or you know what will happen.'

Time passed and after a year Abena's parents began to wonder why they had not heard from her and why the girls had not returned home. They grew thin with worry but still they had no news.

At this time a little bird used to come to a bush at the edge of the village where the children played and he would sit and sing to them this song:

'Abena would not listen to advice,
Abena would not listen to advice,
Abena is now in hot water,
Abena is now in hot water.'

The children repeated the song to their parents who at first took no notice. After a time someone remembered Abena's behaviour and went to see her parents. 'There is a little bird who sings:

"Abena would not listen to advice,
Abena would not listen to advice,
Abena is now in hot water."

Do you think it could be your Abena?' they asked. The parents were sure it must be, but they did not know where to find their daughter. Then the mother, who could not eat for worry, grew ill and died and not long after the father, too, left without daughter or wife, went to join his ancestors and the family was no more.

The little bird now left the village and went to the river where Abena was living in the hole. He sat on a twig above the river and sang each day:

'Abena, poor miserable Abena,
Her mother is dead,
Her father is dead,
And she sits here in complete ignorance.'

Each day Abena listened to the song and wondered what it could mean. She would wait till the python had gone hunting and poke her head out and watch the bird.

One day she called to him timidly, 'Little bird, little bird, is it me you are singing about?' The bird hopped a few twigs lower and put his head on one side. 'Abena, poor miserable Abena,' he said, 'it is indeed about you that I sing.' And Abena wept bitterly.

Looking up through her tears she called to the bird, 'Little bird, little bird, go I pray you to the village and tell my people where I am. I cannot return if I would, for the way is long and I don't know the road. At any rate the python would catch me. Go quickly before he returns.'

The little bird flew away and that evening came again to the village. This time he stood on a tree in the middle and started his song:

'Abena, poor miserable Abena . . .'

There was soon a small crowd round the tree and, when it thought there were enough there, the little bird started to tell them what had happened to Abena. As the tale went on the people grew angry and some wept bitterly, for the maids whom the python had eaten came from their families. One and all swore vengeance on the python.

The young men collected their guns and knives and led by the most intrepid hunter in the village, who had once courted Abena, they asked the bird to show them the way to the river. Under cover of darkness they started on their way and the next day they followed the bird. On the morning of the second day they reached the river.

'You must hide here,' said the bird. 'When the python comes from the river I will sing and then you can jump out and catch him before he goes hunting. So the hunters waited in ambush and soon the python stirred in his hole. He turned as usual to Abena and warned her not to leave whilst he was away. Then he crawled up on to the bank.

'Pam, Pam,' went the guns and the hunters rushed on the python. Soon he was no more.

The hunters called to Abena and, thin and wan, she climbed from the hole and collapsed weeping on the bank. No one had the heart to blame her so they carried her back to the village. The family hut had been empty a long time and she had to go and live with cousins.

As soon as she was strong enough she called all the young girls to her and sang to them this song:

'Listen when mother speaks,
Listen when mother speaks,
For mother knows it all.
If only I had listened to mother
This calamity would not have befallen me.'

As long as she lived Abena devoted her life to the bringing up of the young girls in the village, and they would gather round her in the evening and sing with her, her song:

'Listen when mother speaks
For mother knows it all . . .'

Why the Lizard Stretches his Neck

ONCE there was a powerful Chief who had many wives. He had, however, only one daughter. He guarded her night and day and would not let her go out and about. The people saw her only at a distance at great festivals, otherwise she stayed within the palace. At last, when the Chief was growing old and the daughter had grown into a beautiful young woman, he decided it was time for her to marry. Since he had no other children he decreed that whoever should marry her should have half the kingdom and rule there for him.

The Chief beat the gong-gong far and near and called the people to him. Then he declared through his linguists that anyone who could guess the name of his daughter would marry her. He gave warning, however, that in case of failure the suitor would be immediately executed. Then he went back to his palace and waited.

Now Kwaku Ananse the spider was visiting the town. He heard the announcement and immediately started thinking how he could win the beautiful bride.

Late at night when all was quiet, he climbed over the wall of the palace, and hanging quietly from the roof of the hut, heard the Chief's daughter talking with her friends. 'Ahoafé,' they said, 'no one will guess your name.' Then they discussed at length who the suitors would be, talking of the richest and bravest in the kingdom.

Kwaku Ananse crept back to the house where he was staying and the next day called all his friends and started to celebrate. 'For,' he said, 'I know the name of the Chief's daughter, and tomorrow I, Kwaku Ananse, will marry her. Then I shall rule half the kingdom. I, Kwaku Ananse the Wise, have spoken.' Then he went to prepare himself for a visit to the Chief.

The Lizard had been visiting the house, and on hearing Kwaku Ananse's boast, he wished that he could be in his place. When Kwaku Ananse came out of his room, the Lizard approached him saying: 'Great man, it is not fitting that anyone so important as yourself should go direct to the Chief. It is surely customary in these matters to send a linguist or a messenger to announce your intent. Otherwise the Chief would not respect you.'

Kwaku Ananse replied: 'I am not yet great, Lizard, but tomorrow I will be, for I intend to marry the Chief's daughter. I had thought to go now to the palace to tell him her name. Perhaps, however, you are right. Perhaps I should send someone in my place. Whom do you suggest I could send? It must be someone reliable or there will be trouble.'

'Kwaku Ananse,' said the Lizard. 'I am almost

afraid to suggest it—I know I am not worthy—but perhaps you would overlook my shortcomings and send me. I should not expect any reward but your thanks.' Now Kwaku Ananse had always been mean, and, thinking that this would be a way of getting a cheap messenger, he agreed to the Lizard's suggestion. He told him to go off and tell the Chief that he knew the daughter's name and claimed her hand.

The Lizard reminded him that if he went without knowing the name he might lose his head before he could return and report the success of his mission. So Kwaku Ananse reluctantly told him the girl's name.

'She is called Ahoafé, the Beautiful,' he said. 'Be sure to tell the Chief that it was I, Kwaku Ananse, the clever one, who found this out. Go quickly and I will prepare for tomorrow.'

The Lizard left hurriedly, and looking neither right nor left went straight to the Chief's palace. Kwaku Ananse watched from his balcony and saw the guard at the door let him pass into the first court-yard.

When he reached the gate the Lizard had addressed the guard thus: 'Please admit me to the palace to see the Chief, for I have guessed the name of the Chief's daughter and wish to claim her hand.' The guard looked him up and down and thought him an unlikely suitor, but nonetheless let him into the palace. Soon the Chief was informed that a suitor for the hand of his daughter was waiting in the first courtyard. He called together his elders, made sure the executioner was there, and told his guards to bring the suitor before him. When he saw the Lizard he was very surprised, for no one had thought the Lizard capable of finding out anything. The Chief spoke through his linguist: 'You have come to claim the hand of my daughter. If you are wrong in naming her, the executioner is ready to chop off your head.' And he turned to the executioner and told him to sharpen his sword.

'What is my daughter's name?' he asked.

The Lizard stuttered out, 'Aho, Aho–a–a–a–.'

'What?' said the Chief.

'Ahoafé! Ahoafé, the beautiful,' said the Lizard.

The Chief had to admit that the Lizard had guessed right and ordered his daughter to be brought in. 'Ahoafé,' he said. 'Here is your husband. Get ready for the marriage, for tomorrow you shall marry the Lizard. And you, Lizard, accept this crown and these cloths, for you shall rule half of my kingdom as I promised.'

Soon the Palace was a hive of activity, and there was much work for the palace tailors. The cooks sent messengers all over the town for the best food, and lights were burning all the night long.

Kwaku Ananse heard the gong-gong being beaten, announcing that a husband had been found for the Chief's daughter and inviting everyone to the marriage feast. He prepared himself carefully for the wedding and slept deeply that night. Very early in the morning people came to his house. 'We hear the Lizard is marrying the Chief's daughter,' they said.

'Rubbish,' said Ananse. 'He only went as my messenger. Soon they will come from the palace to lead me to my bride. Let us go and wait in the market square till the messengers reach us.'

Kwaku Ananse went out with his friends into the centre of the town. All was bustle and excitement around them but no one seemed to take notice of Ananse, and he became a bit worried. 'Let us go nearer the palace,' he said. 'Perhaps they cannot find us.'

As they neared the palace a procession came out of the gate. There in the centre, carried on the shoulders

of the Chief's attendants, decked in the richest of cloths, sat the Princess and the Lizard with a crown on his head. Kwaku Ananse could scarcely believe his eyes and was so flabbergasted that he stood rooted to the spot as the procession lurched by. Only then, when the people had passed, did he realise the treachery of the Lizard. He stormed back to the house where he was staying and in front of all his friends he swore the Great Oath of Ashanti, the most sacred of all oaths, that if he ever saw the Lizard again he would tear him limb from limb.

And that, my friends, is why whenever you see a lizard sitting on a wall, or on the branch of a tree, he is always darting his head back and forth. For he knows that Kwaku Ananse can climb anywhere, and if he sees him he must be ready to run.

The Bitter Pill

THERE was once a King, powerful and proud, who ruled his kingdom with the aid of eleven councillors. He enjoyed flattery and was quick to anger, so that most of his subjects agreed to everything he said. Ten of his councillors were yes-men and one alone had courage to tell the truth.

Now, though the King was so arrogant he was also hard-working and energetic and his councillors had their work cut out to keep him occupied. Each day he would think out a new law, each one more tiresome than the other. He would call his council together and ask them what the people thought of the laws and if he was popular in the country. The ten councillors always said: 'Your Majesty can do no wrong in the eyes of the people. They think your laws are wonderful and are happy and contented. The Kingdom prospers under your rule.' And the King was content. Only each and every time the eleventh councillor would say: 'Your Majesty, far be it from me to criticise in any way the wisdom of your actions, but the people complain of the hardness of your laws. They have no heart to work and there is much that needs improving in the kingdom.'

The ten councillors would laugh and say that the old man was not quite right in the head, and the King did not take his remarks seriously—for was he not only one out of so many. After a time, however, the other councillors grew tired of the eleventh and asked the King to remove him as a nuisance and a disturber of their harmony. The King said he would think about it.

That night, when he went to his room he thought over the events of recent years. He remembered how in his childhood the people had danced and sung in the streets. He saw in his mind the smiling faces that greeted his Uncle who had been King before him, and he realised suddenly that it was long since he had seen his own people laugh and sing. For the first time he had doubts. Was it possible that his councillors could be wrong and the old man right? He must find a way of testing them. As he thought a plan came to his head.

Clapping his hands, the King called his most trusted servant. He sent him out to get a large pot of fresh palm wine. This he had secretly brought to his private apartments.

Every day the King took the pot of palm wine and stood it in the sun. Every day it grew more and more fermented. Finally, on the seventh day the King tasted it and it was so bitter that he spat it quickly out. The wine was now ready. It was *odae*.

The next morning, very early, the King sent for all his councillors. 'Come quickly,' he said, 'I have something very important to discuss with you. Do not delay.'

Very soon all the councillors had collected and the King called them into the Council Chamber. Then he ordered the pot of wine to be brought and addressed them thus:

'For many years, my friends, you have acted as my councillors with little or no reward. You have shared my anxieties and advised me in time of trouble. Now something wonderful has happened and I wish to share it with you. This morning one of my subjects has brought to me this pot of palm wine. As soon as I tasted it I knew that it was the best palm wine I had ever tasted. Immediately I thought of you, my councillors, and I have asked you here to share it. So good is it that I have thought of rewarding the maker with a title. But first you must share some with me.'

So the King called his servants to bring a calabash and dipping it into the pot he put it to his lips. So evil was the taste that he had great trouble in swallowing it. But he managed to keep a straight face and then wiped his lips and put on a smile of content. He passed the calabash to the first councillor and asked him to try it.

The first councillor was unprepared for the bitterness of the drink and almost choked over it. But he dared not offend the King so he pretended the drink had gone the wrong way. He thanked the King and said: 'O King! this is indeed a wonderful drink and the man who made it deserves to be made a chief.'

Then the King passed the calabash to the second councillor, who bowed low and sipped the liquid. Tears came to his eyes but he managed to swallow a

86

mouthful. He thanked the King and said: 'O King! the first councillor spoke true. This is a wonderful drink and its maker deserves much gold as well as honour.'

The third councillor drank, and then the fourth, and each one exclaimed at the excellence of the wine. The tenth councillor when his turn came coughed so hard that it was some time before he could add his congratulations.

At last the King turned to the eleventh councillor who stood alone waiting. He dipped the calabash into the wine again and handed it to him, saying: 'You have always disagreed with me but I hope that this time you too will enjoy this drink with me.'

The councillor replied: 'Your Majesty, I appreciate your kindness and I, too, hope that this time I shall be able to agree with all my colleagues.' He poured a libation, said a short prayer, and lifted the calabash to his lips.

No sooner had the wine touched his lips than he spat. He cast the calabash to the floor and turned to the King. 'Your Majesty,' he cried, 'the man who has made this wine and given it to you has committed treason. Do not drink it or you will die. Take my life, if you will, for I am old and have nothing to fear in death. My conscience is clean. I have always kept my oath to advise you to the best of my ability and to speak the truth at all times. Kill me if you will, but if I advise you to drink this wine then I advise you to take poison. It is *odae*.'

The ten councillors were angry for the man spoke the truth. They turned on him and began to scold. The King stood by and finally silenced them. 'So, again, you do not agree. Someone is telling a lie. I am tired of lies. What do you suggest we should do to those who disgrace us by bad advice?'

The ten councillors seeing their chance of getting rid of their old enemy shouted as one: 'He should be executed, he should die. No man should lie to the King.'

'Very well,' said the King. Then he turned to the eleventh councillor and said to him: 'Have you nothing to say?'

The old man stood calmly and looking the King in the face replied: 'Your Majesty, I have served you faithfully for many years. If I must now go to my ancestors, I do so willingly, knowing that I have committed no offence.'

So the King called for his executioners and when they were all there he said to them: 'Take the ten councillors and execute them at once, for they have lied to me for many years.'

So the ten councillors were seized and despite their protestations were carried off and executed. Then the King turned to the eleventh councillor who stood by with tears in his eyes.

'Old friend', he said, 'I owe you an apology. All these years I have allowed the people to deride you. Now I know that you alone have advised me wiselys Go out into my Kingdom and find ten more men as honest as yourself. Then call upon the people to bring you their complaints that I may right any wrong before I die.'

So the old man went forth and chose ten other wise councillors and the people of the Kingdom were happy again. The King met smiling faces when he went into the streets and the town was filled with the sound of dancing and music. Whenever anyone gave bad advice they were met with the cry of, '*Odae, Odae*—the bitter, bitter pill.'

Why the Snake has no Legs

ONCE upon a time all animals had legs, except for the snail and he had his own house instead.

One year the animals got together and decided to make a new farm and to clear the forest. As the work was hard they agreed to do it together and to share the produce.

In the early morning of the first day they all went off together into the forest to start work. At the last moment snake however, apologising profusely, said he could not go with them as he had an urgent matter to deal with at home.

The animals worked hard and well, singing as they worked and joking with each other. It was surprising how quickly the work was done, and at the end of the first day they returned home tired but well satisfied.

The second morning snake again apologised to the animals, saying that his old mother was sick and he could not leave her. And so it went on. Day by day snake made excuses not to work. He used to climb a tall tree and watch the other animals making the farm.

As he watched he grew critical and was sure he could do better than them. So in the end he went to join the others and wandered about telling them what was best to do, avoiding all work himself. As he seldom stayed long in one place all the animals thought he was working elsewhere.

'That is not the way to dig,' he said to the deer. 'Do it like this.' Then he went to the next patch. 'You should put the plants in like this, not as you are doing,' he said to the goat, and went on a bit further. 'You should weed in straight lines not all over the place,' he said to the bush-cow. 'Do it like the duiker.' But he never did any work himself.

In the end the ground was cleared and at the right moment it was dug and planted. The rains came and the plants grew quickly. The sun shone down and soon weeds appeared and the animals were kept busy again weeding the farm. At last the crops were grown and ready for harvesting and the animals rejoiced. The first garden-eggs had been collected, the pepper had turned red on the plants and the plantains started to swell under their broad leaves.

Then tragedy struck the farm. Each morning when the animals went out they found the best of the crops had been stolen. They were very angry for, 'Who,' they said, 'is taking more than his fair share?'

They called a big meeting and after much deliberation elected Kwaku Ananse as chairman, because he was known for his wisdom and cleverness. He let the other animals discuss the matter and when they had finished he said: 'I have a plan but I will not tell it to you as it must be one of our number who is taking our crops. Only give me permission to act and I will find the thief for you.'

The animals agreed.

So Ananse sent them all home and told them to keep away from the farm. 'Only have patience,' he said, 'I will go and consult my fetish and in a week's time I will show you the thief.'

Now, although Ananse had told the animals that he would consult his fetish, he in fact intended to take action at once, trusting that the thief would feel safe for another night.

He went back home and sent his son Ntikuma off to find some barrels of tar in a neighbouring village. Then he waited for the night. When it was quite dark, with only the stars and the moon to show the way, he went with Ntikuma to the farm and spread the tar from the barrels in patches near the places where the crops were best. Then he chose a large tree in the middle of the farm and climbed up into the branches to wait. It was peaceful there and he nearly fell asleep.

In the middle of the night he heard stealthy footsteps in the distance. Every so often the footsteps stopped and the person seemed to be listening. Then the footsteps turned off the path and there was the sound of someone moving about on the farm. They returned to the path and came on towards the tree.

Soon there was the sound of a struggle nearby, and grunts and groans as if a battle were under way. 'Ah!' thought Ananse, 'I have caught the thief.' He waited a little longer and the groans increased. Then he heard the well-known voice of snake talking to himself and cursing. Snake was well and truly stuck and Ananse knew he could not escape without help.

Climbing quietly down from his tree he made his way home to sleep until morning. In the early morning he called together all the other animals and told them what had happened. He warned them to step carefully because of the tar and to take spades with them to cover the other patches up. They all made their way to the farm and soon heard the voice of snake calling for help.

The animals were very angry. They stormed up to the place where he was stuck and surrounded him, beating him with long sticks. At last he begged for mercy but they told him he could stay there until the next day so that he would learn his lesson. Then they went off to harvest the vegetables, and cover the tar.

They came for him in the morning, with ropes and sticks. They built a path of earth over the tar and tied on the ropes.

Then they started to pull. They pulled and they pulled. They pushed sticks under the snake's body, but in vain. At last they decided to all pull together. By now snake was crying out in pain.

They pulled and they pulled and they pulled.

He stretched and he stretched and he stretched.

Then suddenly with a great cry snake came free. The rope slackened and the animals all fell higgledy piggledy one on top of another. They stood up, then collected round snake in amazement. For snake no longer had any legs—he had left them behind in the tar—and his body had stretched so much that he looked like nothing more than a giant earthworm.

The animals carried snake back to his house and in time the wounds healed, but he never went back to his old shape, and till this day he is forced to crawl on his stomach and to hide himself away in shame.

Why the Lion Roars

MANY, many years ago the lion and the rat lived on opposite sides of a river. On a quiet day the sound of their voices would travel across the river so that they knew much about each other's affairs and the wives would come back from the river with gossip about each other's families.

One year there was famine in the land. There was no food to be had for love or money except for a few palm-nut kernels which cost a very great deal. The families of both the lion and the rat went hungry and the wives scolded and chivvied their husbands driving them out to search for food.

One day the lion's wife stood by the river and scolded her husband mercilessly. 'You great good-for-nothing,' she said. 'You pride yourself in being the King of Beasts, in being strong and powerful. What good is your strength and your power if you cannot even bring home a meal for your family. Off with you now and don't come back home until you have found something.'

The King of the Beasts stood with his tail wagging angrily but he had no defence. 'Very well,' he growled, 'I will go off now and by evening I promise you a good meal.' And he turned round and stalked off through the forest.

Now the rat had been listening from his house on the opposite bank, enjoying the whole scene. When he saw the lion go off he hurried along the river bank till he found a tree trunk he could cross, and by the chattering of the birds and monkeys was able to find the path the lion had taken. He followed silently behind.

After going many miles through the forest the lion at last found a place where he could get palm-nut kernels. He bought a huge bag of them and started on the homeward journey. The bag was heavy and he was weak from lack of food so that he had to stop often on the way. When at last he reached the river bank he was so tired that he went down to have a long drink and then curled up in the shade to sleep. The rat saw his chance and bit by bit removed the palm nuts from the sack.

The rat went joyfully home to his wife and family, taking the palm kernels with him. 'Wife,' he called, 'look what I have brought you! There are more hidden by the river if you will come and fetch them. Did I not tell you that I was able to provide for my family. See what I have won by honourable battle.'

The rat's wife was overjoyed and begged her husband to tell her how he had managed to get so many kernels home. He told her that he had fought the lion, King of the Beasts and after winning the battle had taken the food from him and brought it home. The rat's wife listened with open eyes, not knowing whether to believe her husband or not. But she was content and the family ate well that night.

In the meantime the lion had woken up and looked round for his kernels. He looked and he looked but nowhere could he find them. Someone had stolen them whilst he slept and he had to go sadly home and listen to the scoldings of his wife.

'Wife,' he said, 'I brought back with me a huge sack of palm kernels but when I went down to drink at the river, they disappeared, so I have brought nothing home. Tomorrow I will go and find more.'

The lion's wife did not believe him. She thought that he had lazied about all day and had not really searched as he had promised.

Next morning the lion went off again to fetch more palm kernels. The rat was waiting this time near the path and followed him through the forest feeling well-fed and contented. The lion bought more palm kernels and, heavily-laden, again made the long homeward journey. He tried not to stop by the river but the temptation was too great and he was too tired. The moment he lay down to rest and his eyes closed, the rat made off with the food. So for days the lion would go out and find food and the rat would steal it. Try as he would the lion could not find the thief. He grew lean from his exertions whilst the rat and his family grew plump and sleek.

One morning the rat's wife had wandered to the other side of the river and saw the lion's wife trying to hoist the water pot she had filled on to her back. Seeing the rat the lion's wife called out and asked her to help lift the pot. The rat's wife looked at her contemptuously.

'Why should I lift your pot,' she said. 'Does not my husband beat your husband each day in battle and bring home the food he has found. Why should I help the wife of such a weakling. King of the Beasts indeed. He must have lost his touch!' and the rat's wife stalked off along the river bank.

The lion's wife was furious. 'Now I know,' she said, 'Why my husband does not bring home food, I have been disgraced in public by the wife of that insignificant creature, the rat.' She hurried home and gave the lion such a scolding and beating that he hardly escaped from her. When she had told him of the incident he grew furiously angry. In vain he protested that the rat had stolen the food and that they had never fought. His wife called him a liar, and in the end he had to leave the house and go and hide in the forest whilst he thought out his revenge.

When the rat returned home in the evening his wife chattered about the events of the day and in the course of her chattering revealed that she had told the lion's wife that it was the rat who had taken the palm kernels. She laughed when she recounted her insults to the lion's wife.

When the rat heard the tale his face fell. He was angry with his wife but did not know how to scold her, as she had merely repeated what he had said.

'Foolish woman,' he cried, 'you talk too much. Now the lion knows that I have taken the kernels—I mean, now that he knows his wife knows, he will be after us and when I am out he may come to harm you. I must go and search for some juju to protect us. I cannot stay all the time in the house to look after you.'

So the rat went off to look for the juju man to get some magic to use against the lion. He went into the deep forest and at last found the tortoise who was the most famous magician, resting in the shade of the trees. He brought with him an offering of palm kernels.

The tortoise heard his story and thought a moment. 'I have just the thing, I think,' he said, 'drink this liquid and you will be able to turn into any animal you like. The rest I will leave to you.'

So the rat drank the liquid and after a bit of practice found he could indeed turn into any other animal. He set off through the forest to find the lion who, as he had thought, was making his way towards the rat's house.

The rat turned himself into a fierce bush cow and started mooing in a pathetic way. The lion hearing the noise came to ask what was the matter.

99

'Your Majesty,' moaned the bush cow: 'as I was going along the river bank I came to the house of the rat. He was sitting at his door and as I passed I went over to greet him and say good-morning. When I greeted him he appeared to be offended and looked at me angrily and gave a great sneeze. I swear he did not touch me, he just sneezed. The force of that sneeze has carried me here a mile away in the bush. I am bruised and shaken and that is why I am crying.' And the bush cow continued to moan.

The lion looked surprised. He questioned the cow but it always told the same story. In the end he determined to go on to the rat's house as he felt he could not believe such a tale.

As soon as the lion was out of sight the rat took a short cut through the forest and coming again to the path he turned himself into an elephant and started bellowing for all he was worth. Soon the lion padded up and stood looking at him in surprise. 'Friend elephant,' he asked, 'what on earth is the matter with you?'

The elephant bellowed the more and told his tale.

'As I went by the river,' he said, 'I passed the rat's hut and seeing him standing in the door I called out to him in greeting. At first he took no notice but when I repeated the greeting he shouted angrily at me, 'Get out of the way you great hulking brute.' Then he sneezed, just sneezed, and the force of it was so great that it blew me to where I am here in the forest. I am bruised and shaken and hurt by the unkindness of the rat. He must be a most powerful magician.'

This time the lion was forced to think more seriously

of the story. Could it possibly be true? He had never known the rat to act like this before, but there is always a first time. He still resolved to go carefully.

While the lion was going slowly on his way the rat hurried home by secret paths. He went into his house and dressed in all his juju finery, he covered himself with charms, he carried his elephant tail switch and chewed cola. Then he came out of his house to watch for the lion.

The lion came slowly along the path and stopped some way from the house—there was no harm in being careful. He called to the rat from the edge of the clearing. 'Good-morning, neighbour rat, I wanted to have a word with you. Can I come to your house?'

The rat waved his switch and shouted back: 'You call yourself King of the Beasts, but you are not king here. Go back to your own side of the river and don't come any nearer.'

The lion took a few cautious steps and again the rat shouted at him: 'Don't you know what happened to the bush cow and to the elephant. They are heavier than you and bigger. Don't come here or you will suffer the same way.' And he started to walk towards the lion.

The lion backed slowly away. He could not imagine that the little rat should defy him without good reason. He must really have the powers of which he boasted. So the lion turned tail. The rat started to run towards him and the lion, by now in panic, sped off along the forest paths. As he went he roared out in his fear, again and again.

'*Wahu me—waa huu mee—waa huu mee*'
'He has blown me, he has blown me.'

And that is why the lion roars in that way to this day. He remembers the rat chasing him and roars his complaint. As for the rat, from that day to this he has taken to living in a hole in the ground just in case, one day, the lion should discover his trick and be after him.

How Kwaku Ananse won a Kingdom with a Grain of Corn

NYAME, the Sky God, tired of watching the stupidity of his creatures, decided one day to find out which was the wisest amongst them. Sending out his messengers he issued a challenge to all the creatures of the world, saying that he would give more wisdom and honour to the one who proved himself the wisest.

The people heard the messengers in silence for they were afraid to make such a bold claim, afraid of the wrath of God should they try and fail.

'How can we accept such a challenge from the Great God?' they said.

'Surely the task would be too hard. Surely if we fail we will be punished. Better far to keep silent and let others claim the reward.'

Thus it was that instead of a crowd of different creatures claiming Nyame's reward, only Kwaku Ananse the spider came to answer his challenge.

'O Great God of the skies!' said Ananse, 'I come to accept your challenge. For long I have been accepted by the animals as the cleverest of them all. Now I would like to prove it to you, too.'

The Great God, looking down at Ananse, wondered that such a small creature should accept his challenge. Calling together his messengers, and before the assembled people of his Kingdom, he declared, 'Ananse the spider has accepted my challenge. But let me warn you, Kwaku Ananse, before all these witnesses, that if indeed you accept my challenge, accept also my warning. If you fail in your task such calamities will fall upon you and your family that you will wish a hundred times you had never made so bold a claim.'

Ananse, unafraid, bowed low. 'I accept the challenge, O Nyame, and will take the consequences.'

So Nyame the Sky God gave to Kwaku Ananse the spider one grain of corn, saying to him, 'With this one grain of corn you are to bring before me all the people —men, women and children—of the Kingdom beyond the Great River.'

Taking the corn, Ananse bowed again before his God, and returned to his family. His family had heard of his bold claim and of the warning of Nyame and were weeping bitterly at his foolishness. His wife and children chided him for accepting a task that would surely bring nothing but suffering upon them.

The behaviour of his family annoyed Ananse, so sure was he of his success. He went whistling around the house as he hurriedly collected the necessities for his journey. Then he waved goodbye to family and friends and set out on his journey to the Kingdom beyond the River.

As the evening of the first day drew to a close and

the fireflies began to flutter around him in the forest, Kwaku Ananse drew near to a big village. From inside the compounds smells of cooking came to him on the evening breeze.

Stopping a group of children at play in the street, Ananse, drawing himself up, said to them: 'Do you know who I am? I am the great Kwaku Ananse, messenger of God. I am going on a journey to beyond the Great River to do God's business. Show me the house of the Chief as I would stay with him this night.'

So the children took Ananse to the house of the Chief and reported what he had said. The Chief welcomed him warmly, for he was honoured by a visit from God's messenger.

'Quick,' he called to his wives. 'Get together the best food in the palace and cook a meal fit for God's messenger.' And the wives hurried to do his bidding.

'Quick?' he called to his servants. 'Prepare the best room and get water for the bath for we have an honoured guest.' And the servants hurried to do his bidding.

When Ananse had bathed and eaten he joined the Chief and his elders in the courtyard. They talked long into the night and Kwaku Ananse, being a wonderful storyteller, charmed them all by his tales and his talk.

At last, yawning, Ananse turned to the Chief.

'Nana,' he said, 'the time is late and I have a long journey tomorrow. I beg you to let me go and sleep.'

'Of course, of course,' said the Chief, who rose to accompany Ananse to his room.

When they reached his room, Kwaku Ananse went

in and soon returned holding something in his hand.

'Oh, by the way, Nana, God has entrusted me with this very special grain of corn, so special that he has asked me to guard it with my life; but this corn is peculiar, it will not sleep with man, it will not sleep in a granary, nor will it sleep in a room by itself. It must sleep with chickens. I suppose, Nana, that you have chickens?'

'Of course I have chickens,' said the Chief. 'Give me, I pray you, the grain of corn and I will take it myself and put it with the chickens for the night, and you shall have it in the morning.'

So the Chief took the grain of corn and put it carefully into the hut with his chickens, and they all settled for the night.

In the morning, Ananse got up early, bathed, and ate an excellent breakfast. Then he went over to greet the Chief and thanked him for his hospitality. 'Nana, I must be on my way, on God's journey, but before I go give me the grain of corn, I beg you.'

So the chief went to the chickens' house to look for the grain of corn; but alas he found it not. The chickens, waking early, had gobbled it up. He searched and searched in vain and at last, grey in the face and tearing his hair, he came to Ananse.

'Ananse, Kwaku Ananse, you must help me. What shall I do? Alas and alack, my chickens have eaten up God's grain of corn. I will give you anything you want, only protect me from the wrath of God. Take my chickens, take money, only help me, I pray you.'

Ananse looked very serious and shook his head.

'This is indeed a disaster. I am afraid that God will be very angry. But I will do my best to help you since you have been so kind to me. Which of your chickens swallowed the grain of corn?'

'How can I tell?'

Ananse went to the chickens' house and seeing one very fat hen he pointed her out to the Chief.

I am sure, Nana, that it was that fat hen. Look how greedy she is. I know that it was she. Give her to me and as I go I will remove the grain of corn from her with my magic.'

'Take them all,' said the Chief.

'No,' replied Ananse. 'I will take just this one.'

So Ananse went on his way with the blessings of Chief and villagers, and with the fat hen tucked under his arm. All day Ananse walked, resting only for a few minutes so that the hen could peck around and drink from a forest stream. It was already dark when he heard the noise of drumming, and following the sound came to another large village. He stopped on the edge of a crowd and addressed an old woman. 'Grandmother,' he said. 'Do you know me? I am the famous Kwaku Ananse, the messenger of God. Take me, I pray you, to your Chief, for I am tired and would rest the night in your village.'

The old lady had indeed heard of Kwaku Ananse, and elbowing her way excitedly through the crowd told the Chief that the messenger of God was there.

Immediately the Chief left the drumming and dancing, and taking Ananse to his palace begged him to stay with him and do him the honour of attending the celebrations. He called in his wives to prepare a meal and shouted to his servants to get ready the bath and room; then he waited patiently till Kwaku Ananse had bathed and eaten, and took him out to watch the dancing. The drums played a special tune in his honour, and the assembled people cheered him.

It was a pleasant evening, and as the moon was high they sat late. At last Ananse, tired from his long walk, begged the Chief to let him go to rest. The Chief immediately stopped the drumming and accompanied him to his room to say goodnight.

Kwaku Ananse went into his room and came out again with his fat hen.

'Nana,' he said. 'Here is God's own chicken, who is travelling with me. She is a very friendly hen but has one peculiarity; she will not sleep with other hens. Indeed, she will not sleep with men. She will sleep only in one place and that is with sheep. I imagine that you, Nana, have many sheep, and I beg you to let her sleep with them.'

The Chief willingly took the hen and put her gently down with his sheep for the night. Kwaku Ananse slept soundly.

In the morning, when he had bathed and eaten a good meal, Kwaku Ananse stood for a minute at the door of his room and breathed deeply of the early morning air; then humming a little tune as he went, he wandered over to greet the Chief.

'Good morning,' he said. 'Nana, this is indeed a beautiful village and I have enjoyed my stay. However, since I am on God's business I must hurry on my way. Give me, I pray, God's chicken so that we can go.'

The Chief went to the place where his sheep had spent the night and looked for the chicken. Alas and alack, in the night she had been trampled on by the sheep and lay dead on the ground. The Chief was terrified, and wringing his hands and crying out he ran to Kwaku Ananse.

'Kwaku Ananse, Kwaku Ananse, messenger of God! A terrible calamity has befallen us, come and look; my sheep have trodden on God's chicken and killed her! What are we to do, what are we to do? Protect me, I pray you, from the wrath of God, and I will do anything you demand. Take my sheep, take money, only protect me.'

Ananse looked very stern. 'If you had not been so kind,' he said, 'I would do nothing for you. But you have entertained me royally and I must do something in return. Which of your sheep trod on God's chicken, do you think?'

'How can I tell?' said the Chief.

'I am sure it was that fat one with three black legs,' said Kwaku Ananse, 'Give it to me and I will persuade God to take it instead of the chicken.'

'Take them all,' said the Chief, 'only protect me from the wrath of God.'

But Ananse took just the one sheep, protesting that he did not want to rob the Chief. So he went on his way with the blessings of the Chief and people, leading the sheep through the forest.

The way seemed long that day, for the sheep often stopped to graze by the path and they were both troubled by flies. At dusk, however, they came to a banana plantation, and making their way through it and under some orange trees they came to a village on the banks of the Great River.

Stopping three fishermen he saw on their way home, Ananse asked: 'Which is the house of the Chief? I am the great Kwaku Ananse, God's messenger, and this is God's favourite sheep. I have come to spend a night in your village that we may bless it with our presence.'

One of the fishermen hurriedly dropped his fish, and running to the Chief's house told him of the arrival of Kwaku Ananse. Now the Chief was having a bath, but he called to his favourite nephew and sent him out to welcome Ananse and bring him to the palace. He dried himself quickly and was ready to greet Ananse when he arrived.

'Kwaku Ananse, messenger of God,' he said warmly. 'Long have I heard of your wisdom and courage, and I am indeed honoured to have you as my guest. I welcome, too, God's favourite sheep and whilst he is here we will do all that we can to protect and care for him.'

He called to his wives to hurry with the food.

He called to his servants to put fresh water on for the bath.

He called to his maidservants to prepare the room, and lastly he sent his daughters out to cut food for the sheep.

After they had eaten, the Chief took Ananse to the river bank, and because the moon was high and it was a beautiful night, they went out in the royal canoe and paddled gently down the river, listening to the sounds of the forest and hearing the animals come down to drink.

When they returned they drank together, and then Ananse yawned and the Chief said: 'I fear that you are tired after your journey, Kwaku Ananse. Let me take you to your room that you may sleep and rest.' So together they went to Ananse's room.

The sheep was standing outside and Ananse turned to the Chief. 'This is a strange sheep, Nana. It is God's own favourite sheep. In every way it is like other sheep except that it cannot sleep with other sheep, it cannot sleep with goats, nor can it sleep with men, but only with cows. I hope that you have some cows, Nana, or I am afraid that we shall get no sleep tonight.'

'Of course I have cows,' said the Chief. 'It is near here that the cattle cross on their way to the Kingdom beyond the Great River, and of each herd I am given one cow. I have some of the finest cattle in the country.

Give me God's sheep I pray, and I will put it in with my cattle for the night, then we can all sleep in peace.' Kwaku Ananse slept soundly.

In the morning the fishermen, on their way to work, woke Ananse early, and he bathed and ate his breakfast. There was still a slight mist rising from the river as he went to greet the Chief. The Chief was not yet ready, so Ananse drew his cloth around him and watched the river flow by. At last the Chief joined him and after greeting one another they discussed how Ananse should cross the river and how long it would take to reach the capital of the Kingdom on the other side. Then at last Ananse asked the Chief for the sheep, and together they went to fetch it from amongst the cows.

Alas, in the night, frightened by noises from the forest, the cows had trampled on the sheep and it was dead. The Chief trembled with fear. Weeping, and on his knees, he begged Ananse to forgive him. Ananse feigned anger. 'What have you done, O Chief? This was God's favourite sheep, and I trusted you with it. You have let your cows trample on it. How could you be so careless? Why did you not set someone to watch during the night? I fear that God will be so angry he will make the waters of the river flow over your village so that even the graves of your ancestors will be washed away.'

'Help me, help me, I beg you, O great Kwaku Ananse. O messenger of God, come to my aid. It was an accident. Take all my cattle, take my wives and my children, only spare my people, I pray you.'

Ananse pretended to be mollified and asked the Chief which of his cows had killed the sheep.

'How can I tell?' said the Chief.

'I am sure it was that fat one over there, the one with the great wide horns. She is stamping her feet and, see, there is wool on them. Give her to me and I will persuade God to take her instead of the sheep.'

In vain the Chief begged Kwaku Ananse to take all the cows. Ananse took just the one. He went on his way with the blessings of Chief and people, who accompanied him to the river bank. There he embarked in a canoe, and with the cow swimming behind, a rope on her horns, he crossed to the other side.

Once on the further bank Kwaku Ananse waved to the Chief and villagers, and taking a stick he drove the cow before him along the path from the river.

Ananse had not gone very far when he heard before him the sound of wailing and crying. He came upon a funeral procession on its way to a graveyard.

'Who is it that has died?' he asked.

'A child,' the people said. 'A young boy, who was drowned in the river. He was an only child. There are his parents, see how they weep.'

Kwaku Ananse pushed his way through the procession and addressed the weeping parents gently. 'Good people, do not weep so bitterly, I pray. I am God's messenger, and I will take the boy and carry him to God's Kingdom. Then you can be sure of his happiness. Do not bury him in the graveyard, for God has sent me to look for just such a child. See this fat cow? I will give it to you so that you can feast in God's honour. Only give me the body of the child that I may take it to God.'

The parents listened, amazed. Soon everyone was discussing the offer. They saw how fat the cow was, and they were poor people. They thought of the certainty that the child would be taken to God. They accepted the offer.

So Ananse tied the child on his back in the manner that women carry their babies. He took a cloth from one of the women to make sure the child was covered.

'Go quickly,' cried the people. 'Take the child quickly to God's Kingdom, that he may reach there in time.' Kwaku Ananse hurried on his way. The people took the cow back to their village, and were soon feasting on it.

Ananse walked slowly with the burden on his back. It was hot and he did not want to reach the capital of the Kingdom before nightfall.

He approached the town as the women were returning from their farms with headloads of plantain, cassava, and firewood for the evening meal. He stopped one young woman and asked her to take him to the great Chief: 'For I am God's messenger, and I have come a great distance to visit him. See, I am bringing God's favourite son to stay with him for the night. The child sleeps, and I need a room for him.'

The woman called to the others, and dropping their headloads they ran ahead into the town calling to the people that God's messenger had arrived with God's favourite son. Soon a large crowd collected and they accompanied Kwaku Ananse to the palace, keeping at a safe distance lest they disturb God's son.

The Chief and his elders, as soon as they received the news, hurried out to greet Kwaku Ananse personally. They all feared Nyame the Sky God, and felt it a great honour that he should send his messenger and his son to stay with them.

Hurriedly, the best guest rooms were swept. Fresh mats were put on the ground, and the Chief ordered that one of the best of his cloths should be put down for the sleeping child to lie upon.

Ananse laid the child carefully on the cloth, his face to the wall, and asked all the people to leave the room. 'The child is tired,' he said, 'and must have absolute quiet.'

Addressing the Chief he said sternly, 'It's forbidden, Your Majesty, for people to disturb God's son. Tell all your people to keep away, and put a guard at the door so that no one shall enter. Let us leave him to sleep, and when I have bathed I will tell you of my journey.'

'Will he not eat?' said the Chief.

'Not until morning,' replied Kwaku Ananse solemnly.

Bathed, and refreshed by an excellent meal, Kwaku Ananse was led before the Chief and elders. He told them of his journey, of dangers he had encountered, and of his own bravery. So well did he talk that they never thought to question him, but only to ask more and more about his adventures on the way. Many were the tales he told, so it was late before they thought of sleep.

At last Kwaku Ananse finished his tales. 'God,' he told them, 'wishes his son to see something of the world so he has asked me to take him around. Having heard much of the famed Kingdom beyond the Great River, O Chief, I have brought him to visit you. Tomorrow when he wakes you shall greet him as befits the son of Nyame the Sky God. It is late now, and in God's Kingdom he is used to sleeping with other children. On no account must he awake in the presence of adults. The children of God are many, and it is their custom to sleep together. Let me, therefore, see where your children sleep, O Chief, that I may see if it is suitable for him.'

The Chief led Kwaku Ananse to a big hut. There, stretched out on many mats, lay his children. All but the oldest were asleep. Seeing an empty mat in the middle, Kwaku Ananse went to fetch God's son, making sure that the child was well covered in his cloth. He laid him gently on the mat, and he and the Chief crept out. Soon everyone in the palace slept. Only Kwaku Ananse lay awake and listened.

An hour or so later Kwaku Ananse heard voices coming from the children's hut and crept over to listen. The children were talking angrily. 'It is the stranger,' they grumbled. 'He stinks and has no right to come and dirty the sleeping room of the Chief's children. He is old enough to know better or he should have stayed with his mother. Let us beat him and teach him a lesson.'

Ananse heard the sound of fists and gave a sigh of relief. He returned to his own room and slept deeply.

In the morning Ananse got up late for he had over-slept. There was no sound coming from the children's hut, and many of them were out taking their baths by the stream. He ate his breakfast, waited a bit, and then asked to be taken to the Chief.

The Chief greeted him warmly and immediately asked him how God's son had slept.

'Where is the boy?' he said. 'We have prepared gifts for him and soon the official welcome will begin. Did he enjoy the special food we sent to him?'

'I have not seen God's son,' said Ananse. 'I was sure that he was with you for he is used to visiting me early. Where can he be as late as this? Send someone quickly to look for him, for I fear some harm may have be-fallen him.'

'I expect he is with the other children,' smiled the Chief. 'Even God's son must play. Come, let us look into the sleeping hut, and I will send my servants to look by the stream.'

The Chief went to his children's hut, and waiting a moment to get used to the dim light—for the sun was strong outside—he went over to the only sleeping form he could see. He saw it was indeed God's son, wrapped in his cloth. He gently touched the boy's shoulder, but there was no movement. He shook him a little, but still no sign of life. He began to get anxious and pulled back the cloth. Then he saw that the child's body was covered with marks as if it had been beaten. His heart almost stopped beating and he ran to the door and called to Ananse, who hurried to join him.

'There is something wrong,' he said. 'I beg you to

wake the child, for I cannot do so. Look at the marks on his body—I fear he has been beaten.'

Ananse tapped the shoulder of the boy three times. There was still no movement. Then he lifted the child and at once both could see that he was dead. The Chief swayed on his feet and stumbled to the door.

Ananse, grim and silent, stood before him. 'This was God's favourite child,' he said.

Then the Chief broke down altogether. He called to his children, and learning that they had beaten the child he wept bitterly. He called his elders to him and told them what had happened and begged them to kill him then and there that his kingdom might not suffer. He went down on his knees to Kwaku Ananse, great king that he was. 'Kwaku Ananse, God's messenger, spare me. Tell me what I can do. How can I save my kingdom and my people? What must I do to turn away the wrath of God? Take my life, take all my possessions, only do not disgrace me before the people. I will make any sacrifice you require. Turn away, oh turn away the wrath of God.'

Very sternly Ananse said: 'When God hears of this you will face such calamities, such storms of thunder and lightning, such earthquakes and plague as the country has never known. How can you think that your life can atone for that of God's favourite son? Only in one way can I help you. If you like I will appeal to God's pity. If all your people, your women-folk and your children, the sick and the aged come with me before the face of God, then will I plead for you and do what I can. There is no choice. Do this or face destruction.'

The Chief replied: 'O Kwaku Ananse, messenger of God, if you can indeed do this then I will give you all my kingdom. My people shall be yours and my riches I will heap upon you. Only save us from the just wrath of Nyame.'

The Chief called together all his people, even from the remotest villages. They came in their thousands, and when they were gathered together, young and old, women and children, the sick on stretchers of boughs, the blind and the dying, then Kwaku Ananse called to Nyame the Sky God. He called to him to witness that he had brought him all the people of the Kingdom beyond the River, using just the one grain of corn that he had been given.

And Kwaku Ananse brought also the body of the child whom he had promised to take to Nyame. The Sky God had pity on him and breathed into his mouth so that he arose and returned rejoicing to his parents.

Nyame the Sky God kept his promise, as he always does. He gave to Kwaku Ananse the spider so much wisdom that all the people feared him. The Chief heaped upon him riches and gold, so glad was he to escape from the wrath of God.

So Kwaku Ananse returned rich and honoured to his family. But he kept most of the riches to himself, as his family had failed to believe in him.

Kwaku Ananse and the Donkey

A LONG time ago, when he was a young man, Kwaku Ananse made great friends with the donkey. Their farms were near to each other, and after a time they became inseparable companions. The donkey used to accompany Ananse to the farm, and as he was big and strong he would carry back the produce, help him to drag trees from the path, or go hunting with him and carry back the game they had caught when they were successful.

In return, Kwaku Ananse would find food when it was scarce or when the rains failed. He was an amusing companion and had a fund of good stories. Often the villagers would hear the donkey going 'He, he, he, . . .' in the forest as he listened to Kwaku Ananse. If the donkey fell ill, Kwaku Ananse would visit him and soon cheer him up so that he found it easier to get better. Indeed they were the best of friends.

One evening, after work, Kwaku Ananse called round to see his friend as he usually did. But the house was empty and there was no sign of the donkey.

'No doubt,' thought Ananse, 'he has had some urgent call. I will come back in the morning and hear all about it.' So he went home to bed.

In the morning, early, Kwaku Ananse went along to call on the donkey. When they had exchanged the time of day, Kwaku asked him what he had been doing the night before.

'He, he, he,' said the donkey. 'I was doing something private.'

Kwaku Ananse was very curious, as it was unusual for the donkey to have secrets. 'Come,' he said, 'this is not kind of you. You should tell your old friend everything. Maybe I can help you in some way. At any rate, give me the pleasure of sharing your secret— of course I won't tell anyone else.'

So the donkey decided to tell Kwaku Ananse his secret. 'The truth is, I have seen a beautiful girl in a nearby village. She is so beautiful that I have decided to marry her. I have been talking to her and she says she is willing. He, he, he, I am so happy.'

Kwaku Ananse was surprised that his friend, big and ugly as he was, could have persuaded a beautiful girl to marry him. He was curious to see the girl. So he asked the donkey to take him to the village and show her to him.

'Wait a little while until it is all settled,' said the donkey. 'I want to see her family first, then I can introduce you, too.'

But Kwaku Ananse was determined. 'You know how wise I am,' he said. 'Do you not think it would be a good idea if I were to see the girl and talk with her?

Then I can find out if she is worthy of you and if she really loves you. I can plead your cause and tell her what a loyal friend and companion you are, and what a hard worker.'

The donkey was persuaded, and together they set off in the evening to visit the girl in her village. It was the time of day when the young girls played *ampe* and other games at the edge of the village.

When they drew near, Kwaku Ananse asked the donkey to wait. 'Show me the girl,' he said, 'and let me go to her alone. If you are there she will not be able to speak the truth if I ask her if she really wants to marry you. If I go alone then she will speak the truth about you, and I can be reassured that she really loves you.'

'Certainly,' said the donkey. 'That is a good idea. I know that she loves me but it is always nice to hear it through someone else. Go quickly and talk with her so that I can pay her my usual visit.'

When they reached the village and saw the young girls playing, the donkey pointed out his girl. Then he hid himself behind some bushes and waited whilst Kwaku Ananse went forward to speak with her.

Kwaku Ananse was surprised. The girl was indeed beautiful. So beautiful was she, in fact, that Kwaku Ananse immediately wanted to marry her himself.

The girls stopped playing, and Ananse approached smiling. 'Are you not the girl whom the donkey loves and wishes to marry?' he asked.

'Yes indeed I am,' she replied.

'Do you really love him? Do you want to marry him?' asked Kwaku Ananse.

'Certainly,' said the girl. 'He is kind and strong, and I think he would make a good husband. He tells me he has a good farm and will work hard for me and any children we may have. I think he must be quite well off, as he often brings me presents and he looks very well fed.'

'Are you quite, quite sure?' asked Ananse. The girl looked puzzled. 'Are you not his friend?' she said.

Kwaku Ananse laughed. 'He has indeed tricked you. The donkey is my slave. He works for me on my farm and carries all my goods for me. He is neither free nor independent. Do you, such a beautiful girl, want to marry a slave? Do you want to see your husband working for others and not able to bring you back even enough to eat? He is, indeed, in good condition, for I look after my slaves properly. It would be better for you to marry someone like me, who is rich and can give you all the things you need.'

'I don't believe you,' said the girl. 'The donkey told me he was free and his own master. He is such a nice person and I love him. Why should I believe such idle tales.' She turned her back and started to walk away.

'Stop!' called Ananse. 'If you don't believe me I will prove it to you.'

'What proof can you show me?' she replied.

'Tomorrow, in the middle of the day when the sun is high, I will bring donkey here, loaded with all manner of things, hot and sweating. I will sit on the top of the load so that you can see I am master. Then will you be satisfied?'

'If you do that,' replied the girl, 'I will believe you.'

'And if I prove to you that the donkey is a slave and I am his master, will you do me the honour of being my wife instead?' he asked.

'Yes,' said the girl, for she wanted to marry someone with authority, someone with wealth, who could look after her well. If Kwaku Ananse was indeed the master of the donkey then he must be rich and powerful and would make a good husband.

When Ananse returned, the donkey was getting impatient. 'You've been an awfully long time,' he complained. 'What can have kept you so long? Come, let us both go and spend some time with the girl. But tell me first what she said to you. Does she indeed love me as much as I feel?'

'Poor donkey,' said Ananse. 'I have been as long as it took to plead for you. When I asked her if she would marry you she said: "What, that ugly creature, why should I marry him?" She would hear nothing in your favour, until at last I said how strong you were and what heavy loads you could carry. I told her there was no stronger person in all the forest. In the end she agreed to marry you if you would prove your strength to her. So I have promised that tomorrow, at midday, you will come to the village with a huge load, and me riding on top. Then she will be convinced of your strength and will marry you.'

At first the donkey looked crestfallen, but Kwaku Ananse soon cheered him up. 'Come home,' he said, 'for we must be rested for tomorrow. Young girls are often fickle, but when you are married you can prove your worth to her. She is indeed a beautiful girl, and

you are lucky to be marrying her. Surely you can per-
form the task she has set?'

'Oh, that is easy,' said the donkey. So they went
home and early to bed, as they planned to be up early
in the morning to collect the load the donkey had to
carry to his girl's village.

Very early the next morning they went out into the
forest. Kwaku Ananse loaded the donkey with all the
heavy things he could find: firewood, plantain, some
game that had been caught in the trap, and even two

old grinding stones that he tied across the donkey's back. When the donkey was so heavily loaded that he staggered a bit, Kwaku Ananse climbed on top and off they set for the village.

Just in the middle of the day, as Kwaku Ananse had promised, he rode the donkey into the village. Perched on top of the load he bowed left and right to the villagers. The girl and her friends were waiting in a group and started giggling when they saw the sweating donkey and Kwaku Ananse.

As he passed them, Ananse said to the girl: 'Did I not tell you the truth?'

'Yes, indeed you did,' she giggled.

Then he whispered to the donkey to turn round and go back the way he came, to give added proof of the fact that he was the strongest animal in the forest. So the donkey turned round and soon they were on their way home. When they reached the house, Ananse unloaded his friend, who lay down exhausted.

'Did you hear the girl say I was right?' Ananse asked his friend. 'That means that she recognises that you are the strongest person in the forest, and will marry you. But let us not hurry things. Rest for a day and I will bring you food and water. Then we can go and make arrangements at our leisure.'

The donkey was very tired so he agreed, and indeed he slept most of the next day, only getting up to drink the water and eat the food that Ananse had left him.

In the meantime, Kwaku Ananse went to the village, saw the parents of the girl, paid the customary fees, and made all arrangements to marry her. So charming was he to her that she scarcely regretted she was marrying him and not his friend the donkey.

Now Kwaku Ananse realised that the donkey would be very angry when he discovered what had happened, so he had to think of a way to keep the donkey from the village. He thought and he thought and in the end he had an idea for a plan.

When the donkey came to visit him the next day, he found Ananse ill in bed and looking very sad.

'What on earth is the matter, friend Ananse?' asked the donkey, looking worried.

'Oh, my dear friend, I have sad news for you. When I was a small child I had a terrible disease. My parents looked everywhere for a person who could heal me and in the end found one fetish priest many miles from here. He cured me, but said if ever the illness should return I must come at once to him for more medicine or I would die. Now, dear friend, I feel the illness is coming upon me again. My dear parents are dead. but I think I should be able to find the place, indeed I know I can. I must set out at once or I shall surely die.'

The donkey was very upset and cried. Then he said, 'Very well, Ananse, but of course I shall come with you and you shall ride on my back.'

'Oh no,' said Ananse. 'I must go alone. I cannot take much with me and I must leave my house and my farm. Stay here, I pray you, and look after my things and pour libations to my ancestors that I may recover. If after a year I do not return, then you can take my farm and all my things. I wish I could do more for you, old fellow.'

By now the donkey was weeping, but he had to agree to what Kwaku Ananse said. 'Is there nothing else I can do for you?' he asked.

'Well yes, there is something. Please stay away from the girl whilst you are praying for my safe delivery. Wait to get married until I return, and do not leave the farm more than necessary.'

The donkey promised to do all that Ananse asked. Then he went off to get his food. No sooner had he left than Ananse hastily packed up all the money he had saved, all his best clothes and valuables, and took them some way along the path to the village and hid them in the bush. Then he lay down and waited for the donkey's return.

It was agreed that Kwaku Ananse should leave the next morning. The donkey helped him to pack a small bag with some food and enough money for the journey. 'For I am too weak to carry much,' said Ananse.

The following morning Kwaku Ananse left the donkey weeping at his door. He walked slowly along the path and turned to wave good-bye. Soon he was out of sight. A change came over him and he hurried gaily to the place where he had hidden his things, and heavily laden made for the village of his bride.

He had already explained to the girl that as soon as they were married they would have to leave the district. 'The donkey will be so angry,' he said, 'that he may try and kill us. We must leave at once. I have much money and we will find another village far away and buy a farm and settle there.'

As soon as they were married Ananse and his

wife left the village and started out to a new life.

In the meantime, the donkey stayed on the two farms. He worked so hard to keep them going that he had little time to think of pleasure. He sold the produce, and he kept careful accounts so that he could give his friend the money he had made on his return.

Time passed. After one year the donkey still waited hopefully. 'Something may have delayed my friend,' he thought. He waited and waited, though gradually hope died. In the end he decided that Kwaku Ananse must indeed be dead. He wept and performed the funeral custom. Then he thought to himself that he had better go and see his girl in the village.

When the donkey reached the village he asked for the girl. People looked at him strangely. 'Where have you been all this time?' they said. 'The girl was married long ago, and later the husband sent for her family as well, as he has become a rich man. Not one of her relations has remained.' The donkey went sadly home. 'I cannot blame her,' he thought. 'Such a beautiful girl could not be expected to wait for so long.' He thought sadly of what he had missed, and was comforted only by the thought he had remained faithful to his friend. 'Surely God will reward me for that,' he said.

The donkey started going out more and meeting people. One day, in a village market, he met a man who used to trade in the girl's village. 'Do you remember Kwaku Ananse?' the man asked. 'He is a very big man now, and he and his wife have a fine family. I met them in a faraway place when I was trading. Why don't you pay them a visit?' Then the man saw the donkey's face.

The donkey had suddenly realised what had happened. He saw how he had been tricked and how he had wasted his time. Now he was without friend or wife, and he swore that he would take vengeance on Kwaku Ananse, wherever he might be.

The donkey asked the trader where Kwaku Ananse was living, but the man had seen his face and was afraid to tell him. The donkey asked in vain.

At last, seeing he could get no reply, the donkey decided to go and look for himself. He sold his farms and started out on his long journey. From that time to this he has been looking for Kwaku Ananse, mostly in the towns for it is there rich men live. But search as he may, he cannot find him. That is why you often see donkeys in the big villages and towns today. Formerly they lived only in the faraway places and little villages.

At night time or sometimes in the day you will hear the harsh cry of the donkey as he remembers his friend's treachery. 'He, he, he has destroyed me.'

Why the Crow chases the Hen

ONCE upon a time the crow and the hen lived together in friendship in the village. The crow, whose black and white feathers made him quite a handsome bird, was always looking around for something to do.

They were both farmers but at certain seasons there was not much to do on the farm and then they could stay in the village and see to jobs about the house.

One day the crow came to call on the hen and knocked at her door. 'Ko, ko, ko, agoo...' (knock, knock, knock, who is there?) went the crow.

'Here I am, do come in,' said the hen, popping her head out of the door.

131

So the crow came into the house and sat on a stool to talk. 'I have not much to do on the farm, friend hen,' he said. 'Let us each make a drum so that we can have some music.'

But the hen felt very lazy so she said, 'I am sorry, friend crow, but I am not very well. I think I have a touch of fever and I can do no work but what must be done about the house.'

'Then lend me your tools, friend hen,' said the crow, 'and I will make one for us both.'

'Oh! dear, I am so sorry, but when I am ill, then my tools are ill too. I cannot lend them to you, friend crow.'

So the crow went off on his own and by and by he found himself some tools and was soon hard at work on his drum, cutting the hollow wood just so and carving on the outside the usual symbols—the hunter with his gun, the sword and the double crocodile, the lock and the bird looking over its shoulder. All in all he made a handsome drum and he was very proud of it.

When the carving was finished and the pegs made the crow took a good strong piece of skin and damping it first stretched it over the top of the drum and laced it on with cords. Then he put it out to dry in the sun and called the hen to come and see it.

'Friend hen, friend hen,' he called outside her door, 'come and see the fine drum I have made, if you are well enough.'

The hen came out of her door and went with the crow to look at the drum. The moment she saw it she was jealous. She wanted that drum badly.

'It is indeed a fine drum,' she said, 'leave it by my house in the sun to dry and I will keep an eye on it for you.'

'That is very kind of you, friend hen, for I want to go to my farm and pick some vegetables. It is some days since I have been there and there is nothing left in the house. Only, on no account touch the drum nor try and play it, for it is not yet dry and it would spoil if you use it now.'

So the crow went off to its farm and left the drum near the hen's house.

No sooner had the crow left than the hen ran up to the drum. She walked all round it and admired the carvings. Then she thought it could do no harm to give it a gentle beat, so she lifted her claw and went 'tum, tum,' on the drum, very gently.

No one heard and the sound was indeed good. Then she hit it a bit louder and started making up a little tune as she did so, singing softly to herself:

'Whose drum is this drum?
It is the crow's drum,
It is the crow's drum,
If I had hands I would play the crow's drum,
The crow's drum.'

This sounded so good that she tried a little harder. At last she grew so excited she could not resist temptation. She jumped right up on to the drum itself and jumping up and down played it for all she was worth, shouting for all to hear:

'I am playing, I am playing the drum,
Listen I am playing the drum,
The crow's drum.'

The noise was so great that the crow heard it from
the other end of the village—he had stopped to speak
with a neighbour as he went. He turned angrily and
rushed back to the hen's house, shouting at her to stop.
But the hen was too excited to hear and it was not till
the crow was nearly on top of her that she saw him.
Then with a great squawk she jumped from the drum.
As she jumped down one of her claws went right
through the leather on the top and the drum was
spoilt.

The crow tried in vain to catch the hen, but she ran
into her house and locked the door. Each time that he
chased her she was just too quick for him but he never
gave up trying.

From that day to this the crow has always been
chasing the hen, hoping to give her a good beating—
but it rarely manages to catch her. Only from time to
time it carries off one of her little ones.

The Old Man and the Mouse

THERE was once an old man who lived alone on the edge of a village. Once he had been a famous hunter but now he could scarcely find strength to set the traps that provided him with a little meat each day.

When he had caught a rabbit, or a bush rat or when, even more rarely, he trapped an antelope or a duiker he would bring the meat home to his house, keep what he needed for one good meal, put by a little for the morning and sell the rest to the villagers to pay for his necessities.

After the evening meal he put what remained of the meat carefully on the shelf above his bed and settled for the night. Each morning when he went for the meat he found that it was gone and he had to go hungry to work.

Unbeknown to the old man there was a mouse living in a hole in the hut. Instead of going to search for its own food this mouse had acquired a taste for meat and would creep up to the shelf in the night and finish what the old man had left, dragging what he could not finish down into his hole to eat during the day. Thus he grew fat and lazy whilst the old man went short of food.

One day the old man could stand it no longer and vowed that he would catch the thief. When he went to bed that night he chewed cola and managed to keep awake, hard though it was at his advanced age. In the middle of the night he heard a rustle and then a patter and something scratching on the wall. Quietly lighting his lamp under a cloth the old man held it up suddenly and was able to see the mouse in the act of eating the meat. He stood up to try and catch the thief but the mouse was too quick for him and rushed back into its hole. But the old man had seen the entrance to the hole which he had not noticed before and getting a knife he dug down till he reached the mouse and with one grab at the back of his neck pulled it out and stared at it.

'So, little thief, I have caught you at last and now I will kill you so that you can steal no more. Nimble as you are could you not have had pity on an old man and caught your own food?'

Holding the mouse firmly he bent to pick up his knife and was about to kill the mouse when it squeaked out: 'Old man, old man, have mercy on me. I swear I will steal no more. Nay, if you free me I will work hard for you, I will help you so that you will never regret it. Old man, old man I beg you . . .' And he wriggled and squeaked in his anxiety.

The old man looked at the mouse and grumbled: 'What can a little thing like you do to help me? You are better out of the way.'

'I will bring you corn,' squeaked the mouse. 'Many of the villagers have farms and I will bring you corn so that you can eat it with your meat—I will work all day for you.'

The old man was tired and wanted to sleep. He did not feel like arguing so he threw the mouse onto the floor and said: 'Very well. I will see tomorrow what you can do for me—otherwise I will by all means see that you die.' And he lay down and went to sleep.

All day the next day the mouse toiled to bring back corn. But being small he could only carry a few grains at a time and the farms were far from the village. In the evening when the old man came home with a rabbit for the pot only a handful of grain lay on the shelf.

The old man looked at the grain angrily and called to the mouse who lay exhausted in its hole: 'Mouse, you will have to do better than this if I am to spare you. You have not even brought me enough for a meal and I have fed you all these months. I am going to kill you after all.' And he sharpened his knife.

'Old man, old man, I will do better tomorrow, indeed I will. Only give me a second chance.'

Grumbling, the old man agreed.

Very early the next morning before light the mouse crept out of the house and went to call on its grandparents who lived away on the other side of the village. Weeping, it told them the tale of its task. The old people nodded wisely. 'Call together all the mice and rats in the village,' they said, 'together we shall be able to fetch plenty of grain for the old man.'

So the mouse spent the day going round calling his relations. He called on his cousins and his aunts, his great uncles and his great aunts, his mother and father who lived in the next village, and his cousins who lived in the forest. As it was getting dark they all gathered together and started to march to the house of the old man, to tell him what they would do for him.

The old man stood at the door of his house and he heard a rustling and a pattering and the noise of little feet coming from the edge of the forest. He wiped his hand over his eyes and looked. His eyesight was still good and soon he saw coming towards him a whole crowd of mice and rats—big ones, little ones, fat ones, thin ones, black ones, and brown ones. He did not wait to see more. Thinking that they were coming to kill him he fled shouting from his house and disappeared on the other side of the village. The mice waited and waited but he never returned. And from that day to this mice and rats have never lived singly but have protection in numbers.

How Death came
to Mankind

LONG, long ago, before our cities were thought of, Death was unknown to mankind. Only the beasts of the forest knew of his existence and only they suffered from his traps. Death might have stayed in the forest had it not been for the greed of Kwaku Ananse.

One year there was famine in the land. All the people went hungry and grew thin and weak and above all bad-tempered. Kwaku Ananse, unable to get food from his farm grew tired of the taunts of his wife, Aso, and his children.

One morning Aso was particularly unpleasant. 'Husband,' she said, 'you claim to have all the wisdom in the world and yet you cannot do a simple thing like finding us a meal. You have lost your touch or else you are too lazy to work. Go out and find food or we shall know you have lost your wisdom.'

Kwaku Ananse could stand it no longer. He left the house determined not to return till he had found food. He went far, far into the forest until he came to an unknown area. Following a narrow path between the trees he came suddenly into a clearing and there before him, sitting on a log, was an old man. Everything about him was grey—grey hair, grey beard, grey watery eyes; and the arms that came from beneath his grey cloth ended in grey, bloodless hands. These hands were working as Kwaku Ananse entered the clearing; twisting creepers and long grass to make ropes for a trap. The old man did not even look up from his work when Kwaku greeted him.

'Good morning, Grandfather,' said Kwaku Ananse in greeting. 'How are you and what is the news in this part of the forest?' The old man did not reply nor did he stop his work.

'Grandfather,' said Kwaku Ananse, this time almost shouting in case the old man should be deaf. 'Grandfather, how are you?' There was still no reply.

Kwaku Ananse thought to himself that the old man must be quite deaf, so he went up and offered to shake his hand. The old man still did not pay attention and Kwaku shrugged his shoulders and looked about him. As he looked he saw all round, pile upon pile, the bodies of dead animals, some fat, some lean, some newly dead and others already mouldering into the ground. When he looked at the newly dead animals Kwaku Ananse remembered his hunger and that of his family. Again he approached the old man and asked in a loud voice if he might take some meat home with him. But the old man just went on working and in the end Kwaku took as much meat as he could carry and hurried home to his wife. He looked over his shoulder as he left the clearing but the old man still sat there alone.

That night and for many nights after Kwaku Ananse and his family ate well. When the meat was finished Kwaku returned to the same clearing in the forest. Again he greeted the old man and again there was no reply. This time he did not wait to ask but took away as much meat as he could carry. As he went home he wondered to himself what he should do if someone discovered this source of food and how he could keep it all to himself. He decided to go back next time at night to see how it was the old man managed to catch so many animals.

There was a moon that night and Kwaku Ananse easily made his way through the forest. When he got to the clearing it was empty but he could hear the sounds in the forest beyond, and following them he came upon the old man busy laying traps in the forest. As he made new traps he cleared the old and each one seemed to contain at least one animal. These he lifted easily onto his old shoulders and piled up ready to take back to the clearing.

'So,' thought Kwaku Ananse, 'this is a great hunter and he must know the ways of animals very well to catch so many. I will marry my daughter to him and then we shall always be sure of a good supply of meat.'

Kwaku Ananse returned home and informed his daughter, who was a comely young girl and an excellent housewife, that he had found her husband. He told her to bring her cooking pots and follow him through the forest.

The girl was obedient and, saying farewell to her
mother, she went with her father into the forest. When
they reached the clearing the old man was sitting down
again with the freshly collected animals piled nearby.

Kwaku Ananse addressed him in a loud voice.
'Honoured Sir,' he said. 'I have brought you my daughter **as a** wife that she may cook and care for you whilst
you hunt so diligently.' The old man did not reply,
nor did he look up from his work. The girl started to
make herself a hut in the clearing of branches and
creepers and Kwaku helped her finish it. When she had
collected wood and started to cook an evening meal,
Kwaku Ananse picked up some of the fresh meat, and
promising to come the next day he made his way home-
wards.

When Kwaku Ananse returned in the morning the girl was sitting on a log by the door of her hut, looking sad and depressed. Beside her were her cooking pots from which came the delicious smell of a freshly cooked meal.

'Good-morning, daughter,' said Kwaku Ananse. 'How are you getting on with your husband, and did he enjoy your food?'

'Alas, Father,' said the girl, 'he has not spoken to me at all, nor will he taste my food. He has neither eaten nor drunk the whole time I have been here. He just works and works and takes no notice. Take me home with you I pray for he is the strangest old man and I am afraid of him.'

'Have patience, daughter,' said Kwaku Ananse. 'All will be well. He will have to eat soon and then he will recognise you, for few can cook as well as you. Let me eat the meal you have prepared this time and in the evening cook him another so that he may be tempted.'

So the girl agreed to stay on condition her father returned the next day to see her.

The next morning Kwaku Ananse was a little late in starting so that it was midday before he reached the clearing. He looked around for his daughter but saw only the old man working at his traps. He dropped a stick just in front of him to attract his attention and spoke to him: 'Where is my daughter, your wife? I see no signs of cooking. What have you done with her and where has she gone?'

There was no reply.

'Where is my daughter?' shouted Kwaku Ananse.

There was no reply.

Kwaku Ananse started to look round the clearing and suddenly he stopped in horror. There on top of one of the piles of animals lay his daughter, stiff and cold like any of the others. Kwaku Ananse went white, then he grew furiously angry. He turned on the old man and picking up a stick smote him on the back.

'How dare you; how dare you do this to my daughter. The daughter I gave you in marriage. I will beat you till you too lie stretched there on the ground.'

He raised his stick again but this time the old man stood up. He looked him straight in the face and with such an expression of malevolence that Kwaku Ananse backed away. The old man seemed to grow in stature. He started towards Kwaku Ananse but Kwaku Ananse did not wait to see what would happen. He turned tail and fled. As he fled through the forest he heard the footsteps of the old man following him.

Kwaku Ananse ran as he had never run before. But always behind him he heard those determined footsteps. At last he reached the village, screaming and shouting that the old man was after him. The women stopped their cooking and ran to look, the young girls stopped playing their dancing game *ampe*, and ran to the roadside. The old men came from their porches and the young men from their drinking games. The whole village collected to see what was the matter. Kwaku Ananse ran into the Chief's house but the old man stopped when he saw all the people. A look of amazement came over his face as he looked at the crowd standing around him.

'Who are you?' they cried.

'I am Death,' he replied.

'What do you do? Where do you live?'

'I am a trapper and I used to live in the deep forest,' he replied.

As he gazed at the crowd Death thought to himself; 'Why have I wasted so long in the forest. I have spent many hours laying traps for the animals who fell into them one by one. Here in one place are gathered more creatures than I ever saw together before. Trapping should be easier. I will stay with these people and do my work here.'

So Death came to the village and stayed there to lay his traps. No one was safe from them. He would lay them in the bathroom, under the pillows, in the farm and in the drinking bars. People would say to one another:

'He went to take his bath this morning and has not returned.'

'He went to sleep last night and has not wakened.'

'He went to the farm and was bitten by a snake and we found him lying there.'

'She went to bake bread and was found by the oven.'

'She went to fetch palm wine for her husband and fell in the street.'

'They went on the river and the canoe upset.'

Endless were the reasons given but Kwaku Ananse alone knew that it was he who had brought Death to the people, and despite all his wisdom he returned a sadder and wiser man to his house.

The Gift of Densu

ONCE there was a woman who had an only son. One
day they went to dig on her farm and they found a
yam. She gave it to her son and told him to go and
wash it in the nearby river called Densu.

He took it carefully to the river bank and bent down
to wash it, but the current was strong and the river
snatched it from his hand. He did not want to go back
to his mother without the yam so he sat on the bank
and started to sing:

'Densu, give me my yam,
Densu, give me my yam,
The yam that I found on my mother's farm.'

Then Densu gave him a big fish, but as he was going
a hawk swooped down and took it, and he started to
sing again:

146

'Hawk, give me my fish,
Hawk, give me my fish,
The fish which Densu gave me,
Densu who took my yam,
The yam that I found on my mother's farm.'

So the hawk gave him a feather, but as he went the wind blew very hard and it took the feather away, so he started to sing again:

'Wind, give me my feather,
Wind, give me my feather,
The feather which the hawk gave me,
The hawk who took my fish,
The fish which Densu gave me,
Densu who took my yam,
The yam that I found on my mother's farm.'

So the wind gave him a leaf, but on his way a goat crossed his path and snatched the leaf from him, so again he sang:

'Goat, give me my leaf,
Goat, give me my leaf,
The leaf the wind gave me,
The wind who took my feather,
The feather which the hawk gave me,
The hawk who took my fish,
The fish which Densu gave me,
Densu who took my yam,
The yam that I found on my mother's farm.'

So the goat gave him a bottle of palm oil, but on his way he ran into a tree and the bottle was broken, so he sang to the tree:

'Tree, give me my oil,
Tree, give me my oil,
The oil that the goat gave me,
The goat who took my leaf,
The leaf the wind gave me,
The wind who took my feather,
The feather which the hawk gave me,
The hawk who took my fish,
The fish which Densu gave me,
Densu, who took my yam,
The yam that I found on my mother's farm.'

So the tree told him to dig under its roots. He fetched a spade and dug where he was told, and as he was digging he found a bag full of money. So he took the bag of money home to his mother and they lived happily ever after.

Kwaku Ananse and the Kingdom of the Dead

FOR many years Kwaku Ananse, his wife, Aso, and his sons had worked hard to cultivate a big farm in the forest. Now, at last, the plants had grown and the time for the first really good harvest approached. Each day the family would go and cut what they needed to eat, but with so many mouths to fill there was not a great deal left over. Now Kwaku was lucky for there was a famine in much of the land and prices for foodstuffs were high. Not only had he enough to eat, for his land had not been affected, but there was also a surplus.

But when Kwaku sat down of an evening and thought about the farm he wished that he could have it all to himself, that he could sell most of the produce and make a fortune. He forgot that his family had slaved to make the farm too and thought of them only as a burden to be fed. Then, quite suddenly, a plan came to his head. He decided he would die . . .

The next day Kwaku Ananse went to bed. He complained of pains all over his body and groaned a great deal. When they brought him food he only nibbled a little bit here and there and said he felt too sick to swallow. All the best fetish doctors and herbalists were called to his bedside. They recommended this and that but nothing seemed to help. At last, after about a week Ananse ordered that his coffin be made. In the evening, after it had been delivered he called his wife, Aso, to the bedside and with many groans told her that he had too much pain to live and that by morning he was sure to die.

'Dear wife,' he said, 'I fear that when I die my spirit will be restless and I am afraid that it will not easily be able to reach the Kingdom of the Dead. I have had a dream telling me what to do and I beg you to observe my instructions in detail.'

Of course Aso, his wife, promised through her tears to do everything she could.

'You are a good wife,' said Kwaku Ananse. 'When I am dead, very early in the morning, put me in the coffin, but do not nail down the lid for I am fearful of being kept on this earth and of haunting you and the children. Go now and dig a grave in the middle of the farm and when you have finished come again and I will tell you what else to do.'

Aso took the children and they went sorrowing to dig the grave. When they came back Kwaku called them to him and hearing they had done as he asked said, 'Now listen very carefully to what I say. Put into the coffin everything I shall need for pre-paring meals in the next world; put in a cutlass, a knife, a coal-pot and cooking pots and a gourd for my water.' They did as he asked and seeing the preparations were nearly complete Kwaku Ananse called to them again and after drinking a little water whispered to his wife: 'Aso, my dear wife, I am growing weak. Listen carefully to my last commands. When you have put me in the coffin hurry and take it to the farm. Put it in the grave you have dug but do not nail the lid. Just scatter a little earth on the coffin and put some bushes over it. Then run home and do not look back. For one year you must keep away from the farm and not go near it or I am afraid my spirit might harm you.' Then with a sigh he blessed his wife and children and told them to sleep till the morning.

When Aso awoke early in the morning she went fearfully to Kwaku's bed and found that he was no longer breathing. She went and called the children and each time that they came near Kwaku held his breath. Remembering what he had said, they quickly put him into the coffin and carried it to the farm, putting it in the grave as he had asked and pulling a few bushes to cover the place. They then ran home and informed their friends and all the neighbours. There was a grand funeral and everyone expressed sympathy with the wife and sons, and in particular because Kwaku's last command would keep them from the farm and from the food they needed. For a year they lived in hunger and poverty.

As soon as Kwaku heard that his family were out of sight he crawled out of his coffin, stretched himself and went to look for the best foodstuffs to cook himself a large meal. And so for the next year he lived on the farm, keeping it tidy, untroubled by friend or family.

The extra produce he took to far away villages and by working hard made a lot of money which he stored in a hole near his coffin. But time passes. After the celebration of the year's funeral Aso and the family were free to come to the farm again and Kwaku Ananse had to hide in the bushes whilst they went round.

Imagine their amazement when they found the farm had been cared for and fruit collected. They wondered fearfully if it was a ghost who had done the work, or if thieves had taken advantage of their absence. In the end they went and consulted the local fetish priest. He said it must be a thief and ordered them to have a life-size doll made, like a real person and to cover it with latex (raw rubber) and stand it in the centre of the farm.

So Aso went to the wood carver and asked him to carve a figure. He cut a tree in the forest and soon had cut out a life-like figure of a man. Aso thanked him and her sons carried it to the middle of the farm and set it firmly in the ground. Then they got some raw latex from the rubber tree and smeared it thickly all over the figure, and returned home.

When night came Kwaku Ananse went round the farm as usual. Suddenly he saw in front of him the figure of a man. Angry at this invasion of his privacy he strode up to the figure and addressed it angrily: 'Hey fellow, what are you doing on my farm at this time of night? Don't you know that it is trespassing? Be off at once or I shall beat you up.'

But the figure was silent.

'Don't you even want to answer when you are

addressed?' said Kwaku. 'I will hit you then with my
left arm which gives a powerful blow.' So Kwaku
Ananse drew back his left arm and with all his force
slapped the figure on the side of the face. His arm
stuck. Kwaku angrier than ever shouted: 'So you don't
reply and now you try and hold me. Let me slap you
with my right hand and you will know who is master.'

The figure was silent.

Kwaku slapped with his right arm and his hand stuck to the other side of the figure's face.

'So,' he said, 'you would trick me would you? Don't you know that if I hit you with my stomach you will be damaged for life?'

The figure was silent.

Kwaku drew back his stomach and pushed it with all his force against the figure. It stuck fast.

'You are tough,' he said, 'but not as tough as me. I will give you my famous left kick which has sent people to the top of the trees . . . you . . . you . . .'

The figure remained silent.

Kwaku kicked first with his left leg and then with his right and finally was stuck so fast to the figure that he could not move. Now indeed he realised the seriousness of his situation. He begged and beseeched the figure to release him. He offered it money and gold, half the farm even.

But the figure was silent.

So there Kwaku Ananse hung till morning. As the first light came through the trees he saw for the first time the figure's face. Then Aso and the children came to the farm. From afar they saw that there was a lump in front of the figure and as they drew near they rejoiced. 'The fetish priest,' they said, 'was right. We have caught the thief. What shall we do with him.'

Then Kwaku Ananse called out to his wife. She, thinking he was a ghost, fainted on the spot. The children likewise ran back in fear. But Ananse called and called and in the end his wife recovered and the children crept back.

'Are you a ghost?' asked Aso. 'Oh no, dear wife,' cried Ananse. 'Ask the children to release me from this man and I will tell you all.'

'Are you sure you are not a ghost,' said the children.

'No, no,' said Ananse. 'I beg you to release me and I will tell you all.'

So the children got knives and cut away the latex and released Kwaku Ananse. He stood shaking and ashamed in the forest whilst his wife and sons ran round him in circles asking question after question.

'Wife,' he said, 'let us return to the house and I will tell you what has befallen me.' But first he went to the hole where he had buried his money and collecting that and giving his wife the cooking pots, they returned to the house.

As he went Kwaku Ananse thought quickly what he could tell them and in the end he had made a story so convincing that he almost believed it true himself.

'Dear wife,' he said, 'after you had left me in the forest, my spirit made its way to the Kingdom of the Dead. There I was met by our ancestors. They expressed surprise at seeing me and said that it was not yet time for me to come there. I begged to be allowed in and they did in fact let me spend a day or two there so that I could meet old friends. Then they insisted that I return to this world. What, my dear wife, was I to do? I knew you had celebrated the funeral and had told everyone I was dead and I was fearful of frightening you and the children. So for a year I have lived on the farm not daring to come near you. It was fortunate that that rude man caught me and I am able to rejoin you without your suffering too much.'

Now Kwaku Ananse is a wonderful story teller and his wife and children, listening wide-eyed, believed every word of his story. Aso said excitedly: 'You must, dear husband, be the first man to return from the Kingdom of the Dead. Let us call our friends and neighbours and celebrate your return.' Kwaku realised at once what a profit could be made out of his story and told his wife to tell the Chief first.

Aso visited the Chief and told him of Kwaku Ananse's return from the dead. The Chief at first refused to believe but when he was convinced he beat the gong-gong and set off with the assembled people to see this miracle.

They came to Kwaku Ananse's house and Aso called him to the door. When he came out the people dropped back fearing him to be a ghost. Drawing himself up he addressed them: 'My dear friends and you, Chief. It is indeed I, Kwaku Ananse, who address you. See I will eat before you to show you that I am a man and not a spirit. I come to you from the Kingdom of the Dead and bring you greetings from its chiefs and people.'

Kwaku sat down to a bowl of soup and the crowd sighed as they saw him eat. First one and then another drew near and touched him and asked him if he had seen their relations and friends.

But Kwaku wishing to make profit out of his position said that he could only tell them in private what messages he had. 'I have,' he said, 'been endowed with special powers to help you settle family affairs. Any of you wanting help must come to me in the evening and I will advise you from my wisdom.'

For many moons people came to Kwaku's house at night and asked after this or that relation. He gave them messages from their departed and advised them concerning their family affairs. And from each he collected his reward.

And that is how Kwaku Ananse made profit from his visit to the Kingdom of the Dead.